HIS WICKED TOUCH

"Ah, Charlie." Rather than revealing the anger that she sensed flamed just below the surface, Marlow offered her a dangerous smile as he lifted a hand from the wall and allowed his finger to drift lightly over her bare shoulders. Charlie stiffened in shock, her breath catching as those fingers continued to trace an aimless pattern over her shivering skin, heading ever lower. "What am I to do with you?"

Charlie gave a choked sound as the fingers reached the low cut of her bodice. "Marlow."

"Yes?"

"What . . . what are you doing?"

His fair head lowered until his forehead was pressed to her own, his breath sweetly brushing her flushed skin.

"I am seeking to determine if your skin is still as tantalizingly soft as I recall . . ."

from "Marlow's Nemesis" by Debbie Raleigh

MY FAVORITE ROGUE

Lynn Collum
Victoria Hinshaw
Debbie Raleigh

ZEBRA BOOKS
KENSINGTON PUBLISHING CORP.
http://www/kensingtonbooks.com

CONTENTS

REFORMING A ROGUE

Lynn Collum

Dedicated with love to my mother,
Doris Austin Collum

Chapter One

"Durwyn is a complete and utter scoundrel." Baroness Hartford put down her teacup and stared at her younger sisters, Lady Peters and Mrs. Bailey, expecting their agreement. The trio of aging matrons met once a week at the baroness's town house on Cavendish Square to discuss the happenings in Society, their active families, and their wayward brother, Viscount Durwyn. At eight and twenty, he was younger than the youngest of his siblings by more than ten years.

Sophia Bailey, a plump little matron with red curls peeking from under her crisp white cap, leaned over to take a macaroon. While wondering what Cook's secret was, she said, "He is not a scoundrel, Catherine, but a rogue. There is quite a difference, you know."

"You are splitting hairs, sister. His impropriety is the same no matter what name we put to the deed." Lady Hartford sniffed with disdain.

"What has he done now?" Lady Peters asked with a disgusted sigh. Her appearance was much like her younger sister's, but at forty-five her red hair was shot with gray.

The baroness pulled a letter from the drawer of a nearby table. "I have a note from the Marchioness of

Westbrook. It seems our dear brother had the audacity to take a *Cyprian* to the Pump Room in Bath last week. He introduced her as some foreign princess. Why, she garnered no less than three invitations before the game was revealed. Someone stepped on the creature's toe, and she uttered a blasphemy in the presence of everyone."

Lady Peters gasped, but Sophia eyed her half-eaten macaroon with more interest than she gave to her sister's story.

Seeing her sister's inattention, Catherine slapped the letter down on the tea tray, which made the cups rattle in their saucers. Sophia duly looked up and her ladyship continued. "The marchioness hints there might not be invitations to her granddaughter's coming-out ball for our girls after such an affront. Sisters, we cannot allow Durwyn's disregard for convention and his love of pranks to taint Amelia's and Rosanna's prospects. We must do something."

"Do what? " Sophia eyed her with little enthusiasm. Unlike her sisters, *her* daughter was only twelve and wouldn't be on the Marriage Mart for years. Besides, she was in the least situation to be ordering her brother to behave. While Catherine and Elyse had married titled and monied gentlemen, she had followed her heart and married a mere country squire. Mr. Bailey had little patience for Society and all its foolishness, and even less for the viscount and his mischief.

A smile tipped the baroness's usually stern mouth. "I have a plan. We must use our one advantage. Our brother quite dotes on his nieces and nephews, albeit I wish he would show less interest in Alexander." The lady frowned. Her eldest son seemed to live in her brother's shadow. Despite what she might say to her sisters, she would love for the boy to cut a dash through Society, to be thought a nonpareil. But somehow he seemed to lack that spark which Wyn owned in an overabundance. She sighed and got back to her point.

"What Durwyn needs is a wife, and I have just the lady in mind. Meet me at Durwyn House at seven sharp on the morrow. We shall begin a campaign which will result in our brother at last settling down to the life for which he was intended. There is nothing like matrimony to bring a man face-to-face with his responsibilities."

Lady Peters snorted. "Wyn married! What mother would willingly hand her daughter over to him, no matter his title? He'll likely create some scandal and embarrass the girl and her family before the banns are read. They'll call the entire thing off before the ceremony, and think of the scandal then."

Sophia nodded her head. "Elyse is correct. Why, Lord Mansfield is still smarting from the prank Wyn pulled last Christmas at the marquess's house party. Where he got those trained ponies to race I cannot say, but the insult to Mansfield's team was such that by spring Wyn's name was struck from the list of almost every hostess who'd witnessed his joke."

The baroness rose, a signal their tea was at an end. "Never fear, sisters. The lady I have in mind is perfect for him. I have exchanged letters with her father, and he is quite willing to make a match with a viscount, no matter our brother's reputation. All we need do is make Durwyn face his familial responsibilities. He must marry to continue the line. I'm certain he will heed our pleas if we inform him his conduct is hurting the girls' chances to make good marriages."

Lady Peters and Sophia looked at one another. They were baffled by their eldest sister's confidence that she would be able to bend their brother to her will. But the baroness would give no details. She only bid her sisters good day.

Horatio Allen, sixth Viscount Durwyn lay in bed fast asleep, unprepared for the onslaught of females about to disrupt not only his slumber but his life. Not that his life could be called one of routine or calm. The gentleman's father, the fifth viscount, had nearly given up the hope that his wife would give him an heir after three daughters in a row and another decade without issue. Then, at the advanced age of forty, the viscountess had surprised them all and produced a healthy son. Unfortunately, the rigors had proven too much and the lady promptly expired three days later.

Luckily for the widower, the boy had proven a good-natured child and was much pampered and humored by his family and the viscount's staff. But as a result of his upbringing, he had grown into a young gentleman with a great deal of levity and little respect for the conventions that Society imposed on its members. His daring had earned him something of a reputation long before he made his first bow to Society. And things only escalated from there.

Many predicted his courting of danger would see his end before his thirtieth birthday, and there had been several close calls. His yacht had sunk during a race near Brighton, Lord Blakely had challenged him to a duel when Wyn had seduced the gentleman's mistress while the man slept upstairs, and he'd overturned his carriage in an attempt to pass the Royal Mail at night on a narrow bridge. All in all, he had earned his reputation and the title of Rogue of the Realm.

The door to Lord Durwyn's bedroom flew open after

a light knock. That did little to wake him from a deep slumber much aided by the vast quantity of champagne and brandy he'd imbibed the night before. The large room showed that his valet had not attended him. Clothes were tossed about here and there on gilt chairs.

Lady Hartford stood in the middle of the room and called, "Durwyn, wake up at once." The lady had used a borrowed key to get them in without the butler's notice, much to the shock of her sisters.

But the gentleman continued to snore with gusto. Her ladyship moved closer to the ornately carved bed hung with deep green brocade and called his name a second time with the same results.

Mrs. Bailey shook her head. "You are wasting your time, Catherine. He won't be awake for hours. My guess is that his head didn't hit the pillow until just before sunrise."

The baroness would not be defeated. She looked about and her gaze fell upon a pitcher on a nightstand. "I shall speak to my brother at once." She stuck her hand in the icy water, then flicked a spray of the cold droplets on her sleeping brother.

The gentleman's face contorted and a roar issued from him that made Elyse and Sophia back toward the door, but the baroness stood her ground. "Wake up at once, Durwyn."

"What the devil is—" He opened one emerald green eye shot with red. Through blurred vision, he recognized his eldest sister and he groaned. "Cat, there had better be nothing less than a death in the family for you to be disturbing me at this ungodly hour." The enormity of his words penetrated his sleep-dazed brain and his second eye popped opened. "There's been no death, has there?"

"Just the demise of your sisters' hopes for the future of our offspring."

Wyn groaned a second time, then began to massage his aching temple a moment before he ran his fingers through tousled auburn curls. He sat up and glared at the lady. What bee did his sister have in her bonnet to bring her to his very bedchamber? "Can this not wait until this afternoon, when I can pay you a proper visit?" He caught sight of Ellie and Sophie hovering at the door as if they might run like frightened rabbits should he call boo.

"No, it cannot. Your latest escapade echoing through the drawing rooms of Bath and London cannot be ignored. Your nieces are home weeping even as we speak."

"Then they shouldn't have paraded about in those silly bonnets at the British Museum last week." A smile tipped his mouth. Seeing his sister was in no mood for teasing, he added, "Cat, if this has to do with Sandy's new flirt, it's a mere dalliance and the boy is two and twenty. Besides, he didn't know at the time . . ." Wyn's voice petered out when her face blanched white. Clearly she knew nothing of Sandy's little escapade with the opera dancer. Whatever her purpose for being in his room at this ungodly hour, it had nothing to do with the boy.

"My word!" The baroness regained her composure. "Please refrain from calling my son by that silly name. His name is Alexander, and your conduct is as detrimental to his future as to our girls. How could you take a . . . a Cyprian to the Pump Room?"

A wicked smile touched Wyn's well sculpted mouth. "I was visiting Frampton for a few days and things were devilishly flat. How the man abides that watering hole is beyond me. Still, I won a monkey on that little exploit, not to mention the sheer entertainment value of seeing all those old dragons choking on their water. But that might have been the foul taste and not my conduct."

Lady Hartford shoved the letter from the marchioness in his face. "This is what your adventure has cost. Are you prepared to explain this to Amelia and Rosanna?"

Wyn rubbed his eyes, then scanned the letter before he dropped it to the coverlet. A curse hovered on his tongue but he held it out of respect for his sisters. "What's done is done, Cat. There will be other affairs for the girls to attend. I cannot—"

Elyse gathered her courage and moved to stand beside her sister. "Durwyn, we beg you to make amends. Can you not see you are ruining the girls' futures, not to mention risking the Allen line? 'Tis time you settled down and produced an heir and stopped all your roguery. You are the last of our lineage, and between your daredevil stunts and jealous lovers, you are not likely to make it to your thirtieth birthday."

Elyse's trembling tone almost got to him, but his head hurt too much to dwell on her sensitive nature. He leaned back onto the pillows and rubbed at the throbbing pain in his temples. "I won't be coerced into matrimony, dear sisters."

Lady Hartford arched one delicate brow. "So you like being rousted from your bed so early." She looked at her sisters, for Sophia had edged closer to the large bed. "We must make a habit of this, ladies. And when we cannot make it, we must be certain to send one of the older children. Why, I've a good mind to move back into Durwyn House for the coming Season. Hartford House has been in need of a good renovation since I married the baron, and you know Papa always said the doors were open when we wanted to stay." She arched one delicate brow at him.

Wyn glared at his eldest sister with a jaundiced eye.
One of his father's last requests had been to always willingly welcome family back home whenever they wished
to come. There could be little doubt his eldest sister was
not above doing exactly what she said. He would have
no peace while in London. Worse, she was just calcu-
lating enough that she would make certain to track him
down wherever he decided to retreat. He sighed heavily
and wished his head would quit pounding.

The sweet faces of his nieces drifted into his aching
brain and guilt overrode the throbbing. Had his foolish
wager hurt their coming Season? Leave it to the stick-
lers of the *ton* to mete out punishment to the innocent.
Perhaps if he left town for a while, all would be forgotten. He looked up to see the cunning glitter in Cat's
eyes. She was plotting something. Then it dawned what
all the talk of marriage had been about.

His eyes narrowed. "I take it you have some lady in
mind to make my life a misery."

The baroness gave a regal nod of her head. "While
visiting in Devonshire with Hartford last Christmas, I
met just the lady for you—exquisitely lovely, quite biddable, with wealth and breeding. I recently wrote to her
father and hinted that you would very much like to
make the acquaintance of Miss Jane Bosworth to see
how you would suit. He has tendered an invitation for
you to come to Bosley Manor the first week in April."

Wyn glared at his sister's presumption. He'd always
known that he must marry. There were no distant heirs
to continue the Allen line. If he died without issue, the
Durwyn viscountcy would end. But the girl sounded too
perfect. Still, it wouldn't hurt to go and meet the chit.
Then he remembered his old friend Hallowell lived in
Devon and what fun they'd had at Oxford. He could al-

ways visit his friend if the girl turned out to be a fright. He looked at his sister, who watched him with narrowed eyes.

"All I shall promise is that I will meet this Miss Bosworth. Other than that I will not say."

A rare smile settled on the baroness's long face. "That is all we ask for now. Go to Clovelly and meet the lady. I'm sure she will be all that I have said and more." Having achieved her goal, Lady Hartford turned to her sisters. "Shall we go and allow our brother to get some much-needed sleep? He is looking quite burned to the socket."

Wyn shook his head as the door closed behind the ladies. He settled back into the pillows and closed his eyes with little reflection about what he'd just agreed to do. His head pounded too much to have a coherent thought. Perhaps that was why he'd been so biddable.

"Rena! Rena! You must come at once." Kenrick Bosworth hurried across the lawn toward his cousin. At seventeen, his long, lanky frame moved a bit awkwardly as he raced over the uneven terrain. Long sandy brown curls billowed in the wind, giving him the look of a poet or scruffy street urchin, but he wasn't much concerned with his appearance.

The object of his shouts, Mrs. Serena Morgan, smiled her relief at the sight of her young relative waving at her. She turned to Sir Giles Firth, who'd come to Bosley Manor to pay her a visit and, as she often said after he departed, "bore her to tears." "As you can see, sir, I am needed. I don't want to keep you from your daily affairs."

The widowed baronet frowned at Kenrick, but pasted a smile on his face as he bent over her hand. "So the boy has been sent down from school. You most certainly must have your hands full. I have enjoyed our walk together, as I always do, and will call again tomorrow. Good day, madam." He tipped his hat and strode off toward the stables before young Bosworth got to them, likely because Kenrick was too often rude to him, despite Serena's censure.

As she watched the gentleman mount his horse, then canter along the cliff road to Clovelly, she sighed heavily. Their neighbor had begun to call as soon as Serena put aside her mourning gowns for the late Major Morgan. Firth was convinced they had much in common, since each had lost a spouse. But try as she might, he did little to pique her interest despite his handsome features and honorable qualities. Serena had married once without her heart being engaged. She was determined never to do so again.

Kenrick arrived, his gaze on the baronet's retreating form. "How do you abide that prosy gabbler?"

She ignored the question as she started back through the garden to the manor house, her cousin falling into step with her. "Was there something that you need of me?"

"Not I. Father wishes to speak with you. Seems we are to have a visitor, a Viscount Durwyn."

Serena stopped dead in her tracks and turned to her cousin. "Durwyn, the one they call Rogue of the Realm."

The young man's brows shot up and a glimmer of interest reflected in his brown eyes. "Do they? Why?"

"I think the gentleman courts all forms of dangerous pranks, but most especially he courts beautiful women."

A moue puckered Kenrick's mouth. "What can *Father* want with such a man?"

After a thoughtful pause, Serena shrugged. "Perhaps he has heard of uncle's yacht designs. I seem to remember the officers discussing the viscount's yacht sinking while we were posted near Brighton."

Kenrick entwined his arm with his cousin's drawing her back to the manor. "A seagoing lord! Perhaps the old gentleman will allow me to sail the viscount to Lundy Isle while he is here."

Serena rolled her eyes. Her young cousin had managed to damage two of his father's racing yachts in the course of the last two years. His reckless overconfidence was his failing and he had been expressly forbidden to take to the water without his father or one of his father's trusted sailors. "Only if he wishes never to see the pair of you again."

The lad's shoulders sagged. "I have learned my lessons, Rena. Truly I have, *and* I have been studying the navigation charts with Sewell since I came back. Won't you have a word with Papa about me having another go with the *Little Hawk*?"

Serena gently smiled at her eager young cousin. "Be patient, Kenrick. The sloop has only just finished with its repairs, and Uncle needs some time to see you behaving responsibly at the helm before he will allow you to sail alone. Besides, he is still rather mad about your misadventure at Eton."

The young man sighed and nodded his head as they stepped into the large front hall of Bosley Manor. "It wasn't my fault this time, but Papa won't listen." Kenrick directed his cousin to the library, where they found Mr. Gideon Bosworth studying a small model of his newest design which was set to go to the shipbuilders in Plymouth the next day. He stood near six feet and was rather lean for a man in his forties, but years of salt air and sun had aged his skin to a leathery dryness and made him appear a good ten years older. His brown hair was sun bleached in pale blond streaks, and a spray of freckles arched over his Roman nose.

"You wished to see me, Uncle." There was always a certain reserve when she dealt with Gideon Bosworth since her return home. Even though her marriage had not been unhappy, she'd never truly forgiven her uncle for having forced her to wed, at eighteen, a man nearly fifteen years her senior.

The gentleman lowered the model. "Yes, Serena. I need you to make preparations for visitors. Do you remember Lady Hartford and her husband, whom we meet last year in Plymouth?"

Serena did remember the lady quite well. She had asked a great many questions about Jane and her prospects at a small evening affair that they had attended at Jane's aunt's house. Serena had not been fully forthcoming, since she suspected the lady of having targeted her cousin for the lady's own son, who wasn't present at the affair. The fact that the lady seemed to be in search of a wife for her son made Serena suspect that the boy was either a rattle or a rake, neither of which would suit her cousin. Even the baroness was not someone who would fully understand about Jane, so Serena had offered little information.

"I do, sir. Is she coming to visit?" There was no joy in her voice.

"Of course not, 'tis the beginning of the Season, my dear. She has a daughter she is trying to fire off. But she has requested an invitation for her brother, Lord Durwyn, to meet our Jane, with whom she was much impressed." He beamed with a father's natural pride that the girl was considered a diamond of the first water by all who met her.

Serena stood speechless for a moment. Lord Durwyn

and Jane? Why, it offended every sensibility. "Uncle, what can you be thinking? Do you not know that Viscount Durwyn is considered one of the worst rogues of the *ton*?"

The gentleman's brows drew together and he moved away from his niece. "Of course I have heard of him." He looked back at her and added, "As well as his vast properties and wealth. Jane would never want for a thing and would have few demands put upon her."

"Not want for anything except a husband who would truly watch over and protect her," Serena snapped.

Kenrick broke his silence, adding his protest to his cousin's. "Papa, he will terrify Jane if he is this dashing rogue that Serena's heard about."

Mr. Bosworth made a dismissive gesture with his hand and moved over to a table where numerous drawings of sea vessels of varying sizes lay. "You both are being prematurely harsh on a man you have never met. I have asked around in Plymouth about the gentleman since Lady Hartford's letter, and few gentlemen who have met him do not like and respect the viscount. This rogue business is mere female prattle." He looked from his son to his niece and saw doubt on her face, then added, "Besides, no decision has been made by either of us. Jane may not suit him nor he me. I shall judge him for myself when he comes. If he seems in any way ill-suited, I shall refuse any offer he might make."

Kenrick looked to his cousin and shook his head, then moved to stand in front of his father. "Promise me, Papa, that he will be told the truth before any marriage documents are signed."

The gentleman's gaze dropped to the drawings on the table. "I shall make the final decision about that once I meet him." He glared at each of them. "Neither you nor

Serena are to say a word on this matter to him. It is my choice whether to tell him or not before he weds her."

"But you cannot—" Serena started forward, incensed that her uncle would consider allowing the man to marry her cousin and not know the girl's condition.

Mr. Bosworth's anger flared. "This decision is mine and mine alone. You know Dr. McKenney says there is no reason Jane cannot marry and live a happy life. I have heard your objections and will consider them, but for now I wish preparations to be made for the gentleman's arrival on Monday evening. I shall see you both at dinner." He gathered his drawings and strode from the room.

Serena knew her uncle well because she had lived under his roof since she was ten, when her parents had been killed in an inn fire. There was little use in following him and arguing the matter once he made up his mind. Despite all the disadvantages for such a man to marry Jane, Uncle Gideon wouldn't give up his hope that his daughter would be Lady Durwyn.

Kenrick drew her from her musings. "We must do something, Rena. You and I both know that once this rogue sees Jane, he will be like every other man and be utterly dazzled by her beauty. Can you imagine what will happen when he learns the truth? When he learns she is like a child?" The young man began to pace back and forth. "I say we tell him."

Guilt and honor warred within Serena. She wanted only the best for her cousin, but she hated the idea of betraying her uncle, no matter their history. He truly believed he had acted in her best interest when he'd forced her to marry, just like bringing this man here to meet Jane. "It wouldn't be honorable to betray your father in that manner. We will think of something else."

She moved over to the long windows and stared out at the waves in Bristol Channel crashing against the rocky shore on Deadman's Point. "The trick will be to make the gentleman want to leave as soon as possible."

"Leave?" Young Bosworth arched one brow, then smiled. "I quite forgot. You were without doubt the most headstrong female in Devonshire back before you wed. Did you truly race Papa's gig and hit the marker trying to beat Lionel Thomas? Higgby mentioned it the other day when we saw the scarred stone on the obelisk at the crossroads. He thinks you have changed a great deal since you came back, not as much fun."

Her cheeks warmed at the memory not only of her foolish wager, but of the trimming her uncle had given her. "Those adventures are best left in the past. I am older and hopefully wiser." Her eyes narrowed. "But I may have to reach into my bag of old tricks to rid us of Lord Durwyn. Are you game?"

Kenrick's face lit. "Have you already thought of a plan?"

"Not yet, but never fear, I will think of something."

"Whatever your plan, I jolly well want to help."

At that moment the door opened and Miss Jane Bosworth entered the library. Her lovely eyes lit at the sight of her brother and cousin. At nineteen, she was at the height of her beauty, and none could compare. Her guinea gold curls, threaded with a pink ribbon, hung about a face that was flawless perfection, from her delicately arched brows and wide blue eyes to her pert little nose and full pink lips. Serena often wondered how fate could have played such a cruel trick as to injure her cousin's brain at ten years of age and change her life forever. For all intents and purposes, it was as if she were frozen in time, always that young girl in her mind. It had been years after the accident that the local doctor had determined the full extent of the damage and uncle had sworn them all to secrecy.

In truth she lived her life as most young ladies, for there was nothing overt in her actions to show her limitations, yet it was an open secret within the neighborhood by the time the girl was eighteen that she was "possessed of excessively delicate sensibilities." While she joined in many of the social affairs, unlike most young ladies she would not have a Season in London.

"Oh, Rena, look what I have made for you." She held up a poorly rendered painting of the sea.

"Why, it is beautiful, Jane." Serena smiled and moved closer to look at the picture. "If you are finished painting, would you like to go with me to speak with Mrs. Baxter about opening up the Willow Room?"

Jane wrinkled her nose while she put her painting on a nearby table. "The fireplace smokes in that room when the wind blows from the west. Papa's friend Mr. Ackerman said so."

Serena shot a glance at Kenrick and winked. "I know—especially when the wood is damp. But it has the best view of the Point. I'm certain our guest won't mind."

Jane nodded. "I'm not allowed to go to the Point unaccompanied, you know."

"Yes, I do know, and I am very glad you remembered. Come, shall we go down to the kitchens? I believe Cook is making macaroons this morning."

Jane clapped her hands. "Oh, those are my favorite. Come with us, Kenny."

The young man came and slid his arm through his sister's, and she smiled up at him as he led her from the room. "I wager I can eat more than you."

Jane giggled. "Of course you can, silly, you are twice as big as me."

Serena watched the pair a moment, then smiled. They would keep Jane safe and secure here at the Manor. One day a country gentleman who would make few demands of her would come along and fall in love with her and not care about her impairment. Then Jane could lead a nice quiet life as wife and mother here near her family.

On that thought, Serena followed her young relations, determined to do as her uncle had bid her and make arrangements for the detestable Rogue of the Realm. Of course, they wouldn't be the exact arrangements that Uncle Gideon had in mind. A smile tipped her mouth as her mind struck on an idea.

Chapter Two

The high-perch phaeton bowled south along the road from Bristol at such a speed that the Honorable Alexander Hart doubted they would reach their destination safely. He kept his tongue between his teeth, not wanting to appear fainthearted in front of his uncle. He much admired Lord Durwyn. But even at the age of two and twenty, Sandy was rather intimidated by the dashing gentleman, who seemed to be utterly fearless. In his own mind, it was a trait he admired and wished he possessed.

He shifted in the seat and took note of the twilight moon barely visible above the fading light on the horizon. "Do you think we'll make Bosley Manor before nightfall?"

A smile tipped his uncle's mouth. "Afraid of the dark, Sandy, or of my driving in the dark?"

The young man grabbed at his high crown beaver hat when the phaeton hit a hard bump. "I would trust you with my life, sir. I am a country gentleman at heart, but driving on an unfamiliar road at night, does it not concern you?"

They topped the rise of a small hill and Bristol Channel came into to view through a break in the trees. The sun had sunk below the horizon only moments before, giving the sky that purple appearance it took just before darkness fell. The road gleamed like a white ribbon against the dark green terrain, unfolding before them.

The viscount slowed the vehicle as his eyes narrowed on a spot ahead. "Driving at night, like most things, simply requires a steady hand and concentration. Do you see something in the road ahead?"

Sandy peered into the growing darkness. "I do, sir. It looks as if a tree has fallen across the way."

Wyn slowed the phaeton to a modest pace as they traveled down the hill toward the obstruction. He reined his team to a halt and ordered his nephew to the team's head. He climbed down, then said, "Walk 'em, Sandy."

Young Hart was just barely able to turn the phaeton around in the narrow byway between the woods. He called over his shoulder, "Should we go back to Bristol, sir?"

Wyn stood, thoughtfully surveying the downed tree. On the far side there were scrape marks on the road, as if the tree had been dragged into its current position, not fallen. It looked like a deliberate attempt had been made to stop traffic. At the moment that realization struck, two masked horsemen exited the woods with dueling pistols aimed at him. Both riders wore oversized hats and dark clothing.

Highwaymen was Wyn's first thought, but even in the fading light he could see they were mounted on high-bred horses. He looked back and cursed the fact that Sandy had just turned the team to come back. His nephew froze at the sight of the mounted pair. If only Wyn could get at the pistol concealed beneath the carriage seat. He eyed the distance and realized it was too great. There was nothing for it but to stand his ground.

As the pair reined to a halt, the viscount could see they

were better dressed than any robbers he'd ever before seen on the roads or in the dockets at King's Common. There was something not quite right about the situation. Why would highwaymen be working the roads in such a seldom traveled location? If they weren't robbers, then who were they and what did they want?

The taller of the two said, "Are ye Lord Durwyn?" Strangely, as he said the viscount's name, his voice broke. He looked to his companion who gestured him back to the task at hand.

Wyn's brows rose at the question. "I am the viscount."

The lad started. "Well, ye . . . er, we have . . . a message."

The viscount's eyes narrowed as he surveyed the pair. Both were rather slender, one more so than the other, and the second was a good six inches shorter. Something sparkled at the neck of the smaller brigand, and Wyn noted a small silver cross on a delicate chain. If that weren't strange enough, he would swear they both were wearing domino masks to conceal their faces. The one who'd spoken could barely keep his gun from shaking. Was this merely two neighborhood lads out for a lark?

"A message?" Wyn schooled his voiced to sound bored. "From whom?"

Again the nervous one looked to his companion. This time the second spoke in a low, husky voice. "Your reputation precedes you, Rogue. We want none of your kind in Devonshire, and especially not at Bosley Manor. A deadly fate might befall you should you stay to press your attention on the lady."

Wyn's brows shot up. Only someone from the Bosworth family was likely to know of his arrival. What was this about? A hopeful applicant to Miss Bosworth's hand hoping to narrow the field? His gaze moved to the smaller of the two and ran over the slender white hand holding the pistol, then to the delicately pointed chin beneath the mask. The feminine features were quite obvious. Might it be Jane herself?

A devilish grin lit the viscount's face. "And why should I listen to a pair of fools who come out and threaten me with unloaded pistols?"

The taller one gasped and looked to the obvious leader. "I told you—"

"Stubble it," the female highwayman barked at the lad. Without hesitation she tucked the gun into her breeches. "This is your last warning. Your life is in danger if you remain to press your suit with Miss Bosworth. Stay at your own risk." With that she turned her horse and rode away, her companion hot on her heels. They disappeared into the woods.

The viscount laughed even as Sandy hurried to his side. "Uncle, what the devil has my mother gotten us into? We passed an inn about two miles back. Do you not think we should go there for the night and return to London on the morrow?"

"We are for Bosley Manor, Sandy. What would our host think if our servants and luggage arrived this afternoon and we did not?" Wyn eyed the tree and determined he could move it by himself.

"But you heard those . . . people. Your life would be in danger if you go there," Sandy fretted. "No woman, no matter how beautiful Mother declares her, is worth your life. We can go to the inn and send a message that we won't be coming."

Pulling his driving gloves more snugly, Wyn stooped and lifted the tree. "I won't be scared off by a couple of pranksters." Without further debate, he dragged the tree from the roadway.

The lad frowned, then leaped forward to assist in the task. "You think that a prank?" Then his eyes widened as he remembered his uncle's earlier remarks. "How did you know their guns weren't loaded?"

"I didn't, a mere guess. It stood to reason that if they weren't going to rob us, then they had no intention to do anything but issue a warning. Only a fool would have brought a loaded pistol." The viscount signaled his nephew back to the phaeton where he took up the reins and waited for Sandy to climb in.

Once settled, Wyn cracked his whip and set the matched pair of grays at a sharp pace toward Bosley Manor. A smile tipped the gentleman's mouth as it occurred to him that his visit to Devonshire was going to be far more interesting than he had ever envisioned. He couldn't wait to meet Miss Bosworth.

"What shall we do if he tells Papa it was us?" Kenrick asked as he shrugged into his evening jacket in the hallway outside Serena's door.

"He won't." Serena tied her cousin's cravat to hurry along the process of getting him ready for dinner. They were late, and she could only hope that her uncle was so excited about the arrival of the viscount that he wouldn't ring a peal over them. "If we are lucky, they turned the carriage around and went back to Bristol." But she didn't think the man she had challenged on the road would be so fainthearted. He had all but laughed in their faces, even at gunpoint. "And if he dares to come, we will act as innocent as lambs. Come, we mustn't keep the others waiting." She smoothed the skirt of the amber silk evening gown she'd quickly donned on their return and hoped the nervous quaking in her stomach wasn't evident to the lad.

They hurried along the hall and arrived at the head of the stairs just as Lord Durwyn and his companion were ushered into the hall by Winslow. The breath caught in Serena's lungs as she beheld Lord Durwyn in the well-lit great hall. From horseback, she had not realized how tall he was, but he made the butler look small. His athletic physique was well suited to the current fashion of breeches and tailored jackets. Auburn hair glistened with copper lights in the candlelight as he handed his driving coat, hat, and gloves to the old servant. He casually introduced his companion as his nephew, but the boy was nothing like him in looks or manner.

Mr. Hart scarcely stood to his uncle's shoulder and his blond hair framed a face as angelic as a cherub's. There was a reticence in the young man's bearing while he surveyed the hall, as if he didn't want to be there. Serena wondered if he had taken their warning more to heart than the Rogue, as she had come to think of the viscount. As the gentlemen disappeared into the gold drawing room, she tugged on Kenrick's sleeve. "Come, we must go down. We mustn't leave Jane unattended for long."

"Must we? I know he will realize at once that we were his assailants." Kenrick's hands were locked on the bannister in fear. It took Serena another ten minutes to calm her cousin's nerves and they were ready to join the others.

Lord Durwyn, unaware he was under intense scrutiny, followed Bosworth's butler into a large, well-appointed drawing room. He was greeted by his host and the object of his journey, Miss Bosworth. The girl was all that Catherine had predicted. He heard Sandy issue a soft gasp when the girl rose and smiled shyly at their entry. Perhaps this trip into Devonshire would not be a waste after all. Wyn looked forward to quizzing the girl about the encounter on the road.

They quickly got through the awkwardness of introductions. Sandy, so awed by the young lady's beauty, knocked over a small statue of Poseidon on a table as he moved to sit down. Miss Bosworth giggled like a little girl, and when her father frowned at her, she subsided. Sandy was all apologies, and Bosworth guffawed and dismissed the incident as unimportant.

A rather stilted conversation began among the strangers. Wyn put several questions to the young lady, but she stuttered almost incoherent answers and seemed frightened. She often looked to her father, as if needing him to answer for her. Bosworth stepped into the breach and asked, "How was your journey from London?"

A twinkle glinted in Wyn's eyes as he turned his gaze to Miss Bosworth. "Nearly uneventful except for a couple of interesting people we met on the road."

The young lady looked back at him with such a blank expression he suddenly wondered if he was wrong. In truth, his first impression was that Jane Bosworth seemed a rather milk-and-water miss without the pluck to stage such a bold event. If it was not she, then who was the daring female who had accosted them on the road?

Bosworth nodded. "Yes, one always meets interesting people during one's travels, but then that is how we met young Hart's parents."

The door to the drawing room opened and a young lady and gentleman entered. The lady called, "Uncle, do forgive us for being late, but Cook had a crisis in the kitchen which required my attention, and Kenrick was in the library and forgot the time."

In an instant, Wyn recognized the silver cross at the

woman's throat. He smiled, for at last he was certain
he'd found the pair who'd accosted them. Both avoided
looking at him or Sandy. The lad seemed as if he were
about to be sick, for he kept gulping and fidgeting with
his cravat, but the only sign that the lady was in any way
disconcerted was the rather rosy blush on her cheeks.

The viscount inspected her closely. It was difficult to
imagine that she had held a gun on him not an hour pre-
viously. She looked the epitome of the proper English
female in her modestly cut evening gown, with only the
simple necklace gracing her lovely throat. Rich brown
curls were pulled back into a neat chignon at her neck,
but several strands had defiantly escaped and curled
about her heart-shaped face. He found her quite handsome, but in no way comparable to Miss Bosworth in
looks. Clearly, whatever she lacked in looks she made
up for in daring.

Mr. Bosworth frowned at the hurried explanation for
their tardy arrival, but issued no reprimand. Instead he
made the introductions. "Lord Durwyn, Mr. Hart, may
I present my niece, Mrs. Morgan. She lost her husband
in the war last year and recently came to live with us to
be Jane's companion as well as oversee the household.
And this is Kenrick, my son and heir."

Young Bosworth bowed very formally, then moved to
stand at the fireplace. After a quick curtsy, Mrs. Morgan
started across the room to Miss Bosworth's position, but
Wyn stepped into her path. He took her hand and brushed
a kiss across the back. "Mrs. Morgan, if I am not mistaken, we have met before." As he smiled, he playfully
arched one inquisitive brow.

Crystal blue eyes looked up at him with a hint of
challenge. "You are in error, Lord Durwyn, but no doubt
that is not uncommon for a man of your notoriety."

He chuckled at her bold answer. "More often than I care to admit, madam, but I declare no man could forget such lovely eyes."

Her gaze fell to the Aubusson carpet as a guilty blush brightened her cheeks. She offered no comment other than a polite thank you for the compliment. She moved past him without a backward glance and took a position standing behind her cousin Jane's chair.

Wyn's interest was piqued but not by the lovely Jane, who seemed immature and socially awkward, but by the mysterious widow. He returned to his seat and addressed himself to Bosworth. "This is my first time in this part of Devon. The coastline looks rather austere, but I must say quite beautiful."

The older gentleman beamed and nodded. "Aye, sir. In my opinion it's the most beautiful county in England, the moors not withstanding."

Sandy, who hadn't been able to take his eyes off Miss Bosworth, asked, "Perchance the ladies could ride with us in the morning and show us about."

A terrified look crossed Miss Bosworth's face. She shook her head and extended a hand to her father. "No, Papa. No riding, you promised."

Bosworth's face grew rather flushed. "Well, as to that, Kenrick will gladly escort you around. Jane is rather too delicate to be out riding in the chilled morning air. Besides, she has a fear of most large animals."

Wyn was rapidly coming to the conclusion that while the girl was quite the beauty, she had little else to offer a gentleman. He lifted his gaze to the girl's companion, whose blue eyes seemed to be daring him to make some comment. He smiled kindly at Jane. "Then we shall ask nothing more than a tour of the lovely rose garden after our ride. There is nothing more distressful than to be forced to do something you dislike." He winked and the girl relaxed back in her seat and smiled. He turned his attention back to the girl's companion. "And what about you, Mrs. Morgan? Would you care to join us in a morning ride?" His voice held a challenge. "Or are you also fearful of horses?"

Young Mr. Bosworth spoke up for the first time since entering the room. "Afraid? Rena has the best seat in the county. She still holds the record for the best time from Clovelly to Hartland on horseback."

Mrs. Morgan looked disconcerted. "Kenrick, must you expose all my youthful follies?"

Wyn chuckled. The old saw that one cannot judge a book by its cover was certainly true of the lovely widow. "Do join us, madam. I promise not to encourage you to revisit your daring exploits of old."

Just for a moment the air seemed to hang in his lungs as her gaze rested upon his face. He wanted her to go more than he should, which surprised him. After all, she was not the most beautiful woman of his acquaintance— but he suspected she was the most interesting.

"Perhaps another time, sir. I have too many things here awaiting my attention."

"Then we shall hold you to that pledge."

Mr. Bosworth opened his watch and clicked his tongue. "Well, I am certain Kenrick will gladly escort you in the morning. Make certain you show the viscount the two yachts harbored below." The old man beamed. "Designing boats is a hobby of mine. But it grows late. I am certain you gentlemen will wish to change before we dine. I believe your men arrived earlier this afternoon. Winslow will show you to your rooms."

The butler took the gentlemen upstairs while the family remained in the drawing room. The door had scarcely closed behind the visitor when Mr. Bosworth looked to his daughter. "Well, what do you think of the viscount, Puss?"

"He is very pretty, like my French doll that used to be Mama's."

The old gentleman barked, "No talking about dolls or toys, young lady."

Serena frowned at her uncle and put a comforting hand on Jane's shoulder. "You never call a gentleman pretty, my dear. We say handsome."

"Handsome and nice. He was very nice not to make me ride," Jane repeated, then smiled at her cousin.

"Yes, he was." As much as Serena didn't want to admit it, the Rogue had been very nice. She would not have expected such a lion of the fashionable world to be so patient with Jane. Still, it didn't mean he would want a woman with Jane's impairment as his wife. At least she could keep her cousin safe from the Rogue tonight. In the morning, she would again beg her uncle to send the gentleman away.

Wyn lifted a candle from the mantelpiece and lit his cigar. He puffed twice, then listened to the sounds of the others as they made their way upstairs. Moments later the house fell silent and Wyn strode to the long doors to the garden. He stepped onto the darkened terrace that faced the channel to enjoy some solitude and a smoke. It had been a far more interesting day than he had thought when his sister had sent him to meet Miss Bosworth.

He descended into the garden, moving toward a small fountain that gurgled softly. The waning moon gave only enough silvery light for him to see the shape of a stone cherub with an upturned vase from whence came the sounds. Wyn looked back at the manor, and his thoughts turned to Jane Bosworth. She was certainly as lovely as his sister had described, but still there was something about her childlike innocence that gave him more of a paternal feeling, such as he experienced with his own nieces and nephews. Had he become so jaded with the Bits of Muslin that a proper female couldn't hold his interest?

But he knew that wasn't true as his thoughts turned to Mrs. Morgan. She was certainly a puzzle. He could tell by those blue eyes that she had a lively intelligence, but she said little, and on the rare occasion she did speak, it was to disagree with him. What game was the lady playing, and why did she dislike him?

A noise creaked in the night, and Wyn was certain someone had just exited the house. Then he heard his nephew's voice calling his name.

"Over here, you young cawker. You'll wake up the entire household."

Sandy appeared from the darkness, the white of his cravat glowing in the moonlight. "There you are, Uncle. I wanted to speak with you before you retired. I was wondering, are we going to stay for a while or go back to London? I know I urged you not to come here earlier, but well . . . I mean—"

"You mean now that you have seen the incomparable Miss Bosworth, what's an uncle's life, eh?" Wyn teased.

"Oh, well, no, that's not it at all, sir. I mean that, well, have you any doubt that it was Mrs. Morgan and Kenrick who played the bandits?"

Wyn blew a cloud of smoke, surprised that Sandy had stumbled upon the facts on his own. He was rather a good lad but had rarely shown much acuity to Wyn, who replied, "None whatsoever."

"So the threat to your life was a hoax."

Wyn flicked the end of his cigar to the gravel and ground it out. "Not a hoax, but a mystery. Why would they want to discourage Jane from making a good marriage?"

Sandy shuffled his foot in the stones a moment. "Perhaps, sir, it is not marriage they are discouraging, but you."

Wyn laughed. "I am a disreputable rascal, but I have never treated a female badly, nor would I. "

Sandy shrugged. "No doubt they have their reasons, but clearly Mr. Bosworth hopes for an alliance. And you, sir, are you . . . attracted to the young lady?"

Wyn suddenly wished there was more light, for he had the distinct impression that his nephew was more than a little interested in his answer. "She is all that is lovely." He heard a deep sigh. Then he added, "But to be honest, I prefer a more sophisticated woman. No, Miss Bosworth is not for me."

"Then we shall leave soon?" Disappointment edged Sandy's voice.

"Leave? Before we know what mystery lurks behind those walls?" Wyn gestured at Bosley Manor. "I think not. I want to pull back the curtain that Mrs. Morgan has so deliberately drawn in front of us. I shall thoroughly enjoy thwarting her wish for us to be gone."

Serena rushed through her household duties the following morning. She wanted to speak with her uncle before Kenrick brought the men back from their ride. A smile touched her mouth when she remembered that she had urged her cousin to take them to Hartland instead of along the beach cliffs. There was little to see in the drab little town. What would make a rogue want to depart more than boredom?

She hung her apron in the hall near the kitchen, then hurried to the library and knocked. The time was near nine, which meant that Jane wouldn't rise for another half hour or more. There was a long pause after her knock, and Serena began to wonder if her uncle had joined the others on the ride. Then she heard him distractedly call, "Enter."

The gentleman was hunched over his drawing table, several balls of wadded paper on the floor at his feet. Clearly his inspiration was lacking this morning.

"Uncle Gideon, may I speak with you a moment?"

He sighed, then tossed his pencil aside. "May as well. I cannot think properly this morning. Is there a problem?" He pushed away from the table and went to his desk to pour another cup of coffee. After taking a sip, he put it down. "Cold."

"I shall order more." Serena took the tray to the door and ordered a passing footman to bring fresh coffee. She wanted her uncle in a receptive mood for their conversation.

"Is Durwyn back from his ride? I was thinking I would take him to the wharf and—"

"Uncle, please don't continue with this madness of trying to wed Jane to this man. She is ill equipped to live in London."

The gentleman puffed up, folding his arms across his chest. "Serena, we have had this conversation before. At least give us the time to get to know him. Why, he was all that was kind to her at dinner when she spilled her wine." Mr. Bosworth frowned as the memory replayed in his thoughts. "Perhaps it is best we do not allow her

any more spirits when we dine. She was rather boister-
ous after the meal."

Serena shook her head. "Perhaps I should have allowed
her to continue her little dance. Then the gentleman might
fully understand the task involved with supervising Jane."
Seeing the belligerent expression on her uncle's face, she
added, "At the very least, tell him what he would face.
There is no point in wasting his time dangling after a girl
who will not suit him in the least. She deserves someone
who can love her despite her impairment."

He walked to the window and looked out, pondering
his niece's request. At last he looked back at her. "I
promised I would tell him should he make her an offer,
and I see no reason to change my mind. You are too full
of romantic notions, Serena. Most gentlemen of the *ton*
want a beautiful wife who looks good on their arm and
can provide them with an heir. Jane is fully capable of
serving that function. She will make a doting mother."

"You make her sound little better than a—"

"Enough. The subject is closed. You would do better
to occupy yourself with finding something to keep his
lordship entertained while he is in Devon. That's it, we
must have a party! Jane dances quite well. Arrange
something small and intimate where a few couples can
take to the floor."

"But, Uncle—"

He held up his finger to silence her. "I expect you to
arrange a party. Leave my daughter's welfare to me,
madam." He looked about a moment, then announced,
"I must go down and speak with Sewell about how the
new yacht sails." He pointed at her. "A party on . . . say,
Friday. Yes, Friday will be just the thing." He strode
from the room just as the footman arrived with the new
coffee.

Serena thanked the footman, then poured herself a cup and sipped the bitter liquid. It very much suited her mood. If her uncle was blinded by ambition, she was not. Jane and Lord Durwyn were no more suited than Prinny and Princess Caroline had proven to be. But it would never do to openly defy Uncle Gideon, so she must plan a party. The trick would be to make it an affair that Durwyn would detest. She thought a moment. Then a smile lit her face. She would invite only a select few of the neighbors. Without the least hesitation, she sat down at her uncle's desk and made out the guest list.

A knock sounded on the door just as she put the last name on the list. She called, "Enter."

Abby, the maid charged with taking care of Jane, stepped into the room alone and Serena frowned. "Mrs. Morgan, I took Miss Jane 'er cocoa and she weren't in 'er bed. I've looked from one end of the 'ouse to the other and can't find 'er."

Serena's heart plummeted. Jane was very much a creature of habit. Where could she be? "Did she say anything when you put her to bed last night?"

A tiny crease appeared on the girl's face. "Well, she was chattering about the gentlemen so. I didn't think she would sleep, so I told her about Molly and her new kittens. Told her I would take her to see 'em after nuncheon."

"And where is the cat?" Serena was certain that Jane had gone in search of the new litter. She adored kittens.

"In the carriage house, ma'am."

Serena handed the guest list to the maid. "Take this to Mrs. Wells and inform her it's the numbers for the party uncle wishes on Friday. Tell her I will join her later to discuss the menu." The widow then hurried out the library door toward the stables. Her step hastened when the thought suddenly occurred to her that if the maid hadn't helped her dress, Jane might be at the carriage house in her wrapper and nightcap. How would she explain that to the gentlemen should they return and find her?

As she exited the garden, Serena froze. Coming across the drive with Jane in tow were Lord Durwyn, Mr. Hart, and Kenrick. Serena's gaze skimmed her cousin quickly and she determined that thankfully her cousin had taken the time to slip on one of the old gowns that she used when she helped cut flowers in the gardens. The only thing which might cause the gentlemen to wonder about the girl was that her hair was still tousled from her nightcap and hanging down her back.

Jane dropped the viscount's arm and dashed to Serena. "Molly has had eight kittens this time. Two white, one black, and the others all gray tabbies. Please ask Papa if I might keep one of the white ones in the house."

"I will ask, but you know what your father says about animals in the house." Just then the gentlemen arrived and greetings were exchanged. Hoping to send her cousin inside without too much attention being drawn to her attire, Serena said, "Jane, I think Abby is looking for you."

Jane's eyes grew wide as she looked down at her gown, which had dirty stains on the front. To Serena's relief, she politely excused herself and hurried away. Kenrick then invited Sandy to the gun room to show the young man a rifle that his father had purchased from a traveler just arrived from America. Young Hart invited his uncle to join them, but the viscount politely declined. The young men departed, leaving Serena and the gentleman standing in the garden.

Lord Durwyn smiled at her. "Miss Bosworth is quite an original. Would her father object to our taking her to Clovelly one day while we are here?"

Serena decided that polite banter was not what was

needed at this juncture. "You must ask my uncle. How long do you intend to stay, my lord?"

The gentleman's brow arched at her plain speaking. A sudden twinkle came into his eyes.

"Why, one cannot come to such an important decision overnight, ma'am. Having been married, you must know. I think it very important that I get to know Miss Bosworth and she me. We must determine if we shall suit. I think a month will do."

Unable to explain why, Serena got the distinct impression that he was trying to provoke her. She had no doubt that he knew that she and Kenrick had waylaid him on the road and tried to scare him off. Was he staying because he truly was interested in Jane or because he wanted to irritate her? Well, she wouldn't play into his hand.

"You are most welcome to stay as long as need be. We have a great many things planned to entertain you. Even now I am making arrangements for a party in your honor on Friday. All my uncle's *old* friends are coming to make your acquaintance and play whist—chicken stakes only, of course."

If she had hoped to disconcert the viscount, she was doomed to disappointment. He smiled at her. "I must admit I could use some quiet entertainment. I can spend the entire evening with Miss Bosworth, for surely she does not play cards."

Serena gritted her teeth in frustration but was not ready to give up. "Well, as to that, I'm certain you will have to stand in line to speak with Jane. All the local gentlemen vie for her attention."

Before his lordship could respond, Winslow appeared on the terrace to summon the gentlemen to breakfast.

"Do join us, Mrs. Morgan." He offered her his arm.

Serena hesitated a moment, then allowed her fingers

to lightly touch him. A strange tingle seemed to race up her arm when her hand closed over the sleeve of his blue jacket. For the first time since the viscount had come, it suddenly occurred to her that she might be susceptible to his masculine charm. She hurriedly made an excuse as they headed back toward the manor. "I dined earlier, sir. I have much to do to plan for the party and will leave you to enjoy your meal with the others."

During the walk back, he questioned her about her life following the drum with her late husband. She spoke of her stay in Lisbon and her love of the Portuguese climate, which he agreed was all that was delightful.

At the breakfast parlor door, Lord Durwyn lifted her hand from his arm and kissed it with practiced savoir faire. He mockingly said, "You have made us feel so welcome, Mrs. Morgan, I fear we shall never wish to go back to London." He stepped into the breakfast room, where Mr. Bosworth, Kenrick, and Mr. Hart were already seated enjoying their meal.

When the door closed, Serena sighed with frustration. He had all but challenged her to drive him away. With her cousin's welfare in mind, she hurried down to the kitchen to continue her plans for the most boring party in Devonshire.

Chapter Three

"By the gods, girl, what the deuce were you about to invite this miserable lot to a party?" Gideon Bosworth whispered into his niece's ear. "I could have gone to the graveyard and recruited a livelier bunch."

A gracious smile rested on Serena's lips as her gaze centered on Jane. Her cousin sat at the opposite end of the Long Gallery engaged in a game of bagatelle, young Mr. Hart at her side encouraging her play. Serena's smile widened to amusement when she noted Lord Durwyn a few feet away being educated on the newest ways to drain fields. John Davis, a young squire who'd recently inherited a nearby estate, was mad for all things agricultural. If his dull discourse didn't send the viscount running, nothing would. She turned to her uncle. "You said you wanted a party, sir. I gave you a party. These are our neighbors."

"Oh, good heaven," Mr. Bosworth cried, "that bore Davis will have the viscount wanting to return to London tonight if he has to listen to all that drivel about irrigation runs and turnips. I must go rescue our guest of honor, but don't think we are finished with this conversation, madam."

Her uncle worked his way through the card tables and

clamped a hand over Mr. Davis's arm. Serena couldn't hear the words, but she was certain that her uncle had distracted him, since he was able to draw the young man away.

Lord Durwyn caught her gaze at that moment. She smiled blandly at him and his eyes twinkled with amusement. It was plain to see that he was aware of what she had done. A bemused smile on his face, he started across the room. Serena's heart grew a bit rapid at the thought of crossing swords with the gentleman, but before he was halfway to her, Mrs. Baker stepped into his path. A tingle of disappointment filled Serena at the distraction. The old lady introduced him to her niece, Miss Anna Baker. The girl was a pretty little red-head who was in Clovelly to visit her aunt for a month. The young lady hadn't been included in the invitation, Serena not knowing of her existence, but Mrs. Baker had brought her along, saying, "What is one more after all, my dear Mrs. Morgan?"

Not wanting to be caught staring at the gentleman, Serena moved about the room, making certain that all the guests where properly entertained. All the while her thoughts were on the viscount behind her. The week had been the most interesting she'd spent since arriving back at Bosley Manor. She hadn't changed her mind about him being the right man for Jane, but she couldn't deny that there was far more to him than his reputation. He had been perfectly agreeable to any plan suggested to him, whether it was riding, sailing, or merely walking in the garden with Jane. He never seemed to get bored or tired or short of temper—not even when Serena had tried his patience with the maids delivering cold shaving water, or when she had Cook leave his capon on the spit an extra ten minutes, which had left it roasted to a crisp. He would always give her that knowing smile which made her every nerve tingle.

A hand clamped over Serena's arm, bringing her out of her revery. Kenrick whispered, "Rena, why didn't you warn me what you had planned?"

"And leave me here to face our guests alone?" She smiled at Mr. Correll, who lifted his goblet at her before he winked broadly, then took a sip from his fourth glass of claret. Perhaps she should warn Winslow to limit the spirits for the old gentleman.

"Well, the least you could have done was invite a few young ladies to make the night bearable." Kenrick's gaze raked the row of gray-haired women and plump matrons playing cards or sitting in small groups gossiping. No doubt their subject was his lordship, since he had charmed nearly all of them.

"There is Miss Baker." Serena looked back to see the young lady hanging on Lord Durwyn's every word.

"Her! All she wanted to talk about was The Rogue," Kenrick said sulkily.

At that moment, Mrs. Hammond played a chord on the piano to encourage those who wanted to dance that the time was at hand. Serena had persuaded her to play earlier.

Kenrick straightened. "I'm going to my room before I have to have my toes tread on by one of these old dragons." He turned and slipped from the room.

Serena scarcely noted Kenrick's departure as she watched the viscount bow over Miss Baker's hand then usher her to the opposite side of the room where the furniture had been removed for dancing. Serena couldn't understand why she wasn't happier that he wasn't dancing with Jane, yet there was a strange feeling in her stomach as she watched the redhead take his hand and smile up at him. Several older couples joined the line, along with Jane and Mr. Hart.

"My dear Mrs. Morgan, would you care to dance?" Sir Giles appeared at Serena's side.

"Thank you, but I do not intend to dance this evening, since I must act as Uncle's hostess, sir."

"An excellent idea, my dear madam, or you might have to subject yourself to Lord Durwyn's unwanted attentions." The baronet lifted his quizzing glass to eye the viscount as the music began.

Serena stiffened. "I don't believe his lordship's conduct has been in any way improper, sir." She didn't understand why she defended the gentleman, but the baronet's smug superiority made her angry.

"But his reputation, my dear. I cannot imagine what Mr. Bosworth was thinking to invite such a scoundrel to his home."

"Lord Durwyn is good *ton,* sir. He is invited everywhere. One shouldn't listen to scurrilous gossip, Sir Giles. Pray excuse me, but I see Lady Amberly is signaling me." Serena hurried across the room, berating herself. Had she not done exactly the same thing she had accused the baronet of doing? The viscount had been more than kind to Jane this week and hadn't said a thing about the girl's more childish quirks, such as a preference for spillikins and bagatelle, children's games, instead of whist or piquet, or her lack of riding skills, or her penchant for chasing butterflies in the garden.

After listening to Lady Amberly's praises of the London gentlemen, Serena moved to speak with many of the other ladies who chose not to play or dance. Several times Sir Giles approached and tried to apologize. At last she let him have his say, hoping to put an end to his trailing presence. She accepted his apology but hurriedly brushed him off with the excuse of her duties to see the guests' welfare. Mr. Correll made a ruckus when Winslow was slow refilling his glass, and Uncle Gideon glared at her every time she looked his way.

Despite her hostess obligations, she noted that the viscount danced with Jane only once, then again with Miss Baker. In fact, as the evening wore on, the red-haired flirt was rarely from the gentleman's side, and he didn't seem to mind a bit. Her plan had been, while not an utter failure, not what she had hoped. The party was proving more a torture for her than for him, thanks to Miss Baker's wiles. Thankfully, Jane seemed not to notice the viscount's lack of attention, being much entertained by Mr. Hart and several other single gentlemen.

As with most country parties, and especially one in which the median age of the guests was near sixty, people began to take their leave near eleven. Serena sent Jane up to bed when the first guests had called for their wraps. Forced to remain at her post of hostess, Serena bid each departing guest good night. Most everyone was gone when Mr. Correll arrived to linger over her hand, his words slurred.

"Won'erful party, Mrs. Morgan. Bosworth always did have an excellent cellar." He kissed her hand and she couldn't wait to remove the glove, where a damp spot showed. She smiled politely as he swayed and repeated, "Won'erful night."

He continued to clutch her hand and sway, his eyelids drooping. Serena gently tried to pry his fingers from hers. "Mr. Correll, I believe your carriage is waiting."

His eyes popped open, and again he lifted her hand to press another damp kiss upon the back. "Handsome woman, Mrs. Morgan."

"Sir," Serena said, tugging her hand in an attempt to free it, "the party is over."

Just as she was about to call for the butler's assistance, Lord Durwyn appeared at her side. He unclasped the old gentleman's grip and turned him toward the front door. "It was a pleasure to make your acquaintance, Mr. Correll."

Honored to have the viscount take such notice of him, the old gentleman allowed himself to be escorted to his carriage. "My lord, the honor is all mine. You would be welcome at Correll Court anytime you are in Devonshire."

Serena watched the viscount say all that was proper to the intoxicated gentleman before he stepped back to allow the footmen to help the man into his carriage.

The carriage pulled away and Lord Durwyn returned to Serena's side. "Delightful party, madam."

"Rubbish!" Serena said, then smiled.

"You didn't enjoy yourself?" He quirked a smile at her, his green eyes twinkling.

"I suppose having a tooth extracted would have been a bit more painful, but not much."

Durwyn lifted the hand that had escaped Correll's mauling to his lips and softly kissed the surface. The look in his eyes made Serena's knees grow weak. "Poor dear, would that I could properly kiss you and make it all better—but I fear Sir Giles might take me to task."

"Sir Giles has nothing to say about my affairs. Where did you—"

The viscount straightened and arched an auburn brow.

From across the hall, Mr. Bosworth interrupted. "Serena, I would have a word with you. You mustn't keep Lord Durwyn up all night gabbling."

Her cheeks warmed and the viscount winked, then bowed to her before he went over and informed his host that he had thoroughly enjoyed the evening. Gideon Bosworth eyed him doubtfully for a moment, then accepted his praise and bid him good night.

Serena spent the next ten minutes receiving a rare trimming for having invited the oldest neighbors they knew. "Lucky for you, madam, that Mrs. Baker brought that saucy niece of hers or the party would have been a dead bore for the gentlemen."

It was late, so Serena didn't bother to remind her uncle that the viscount had spent far more time with the little redhead than with Jane. That fact alone should have made Serena happy, but as she made her way up to bed, she was rather blue deviled. She attributed the feeling to the dreadful party she'd just presided over and not the viscount's flirtion with Miss Baker.

Saturday morning dawned bright and sunny and, as was their ususal habit, Serena and Jane rose to cut flowers to take to the parish church in Clovelly for Sunday services. They worked in the sheltered garden nearest the manor, since the new spring growth had produced an abundance of yellow daffodils and purple irises.

The gentlemen slept late and came down to breakfast while Serena and Jane wandered just beyond the breakfast parlor windows, selecting the perfect blooms. Within fifteen minutes, Kenrick, Sandy, and the viscount had joined the ladies to take over the footmen's duties of holding the baskets.

Kenrick took a flower from his sister and laid it in the basket. "We thought we might join you this morning,

Rena. Sandy and his lordship haven't seen Clovelly as yet."

Serena halted her task and looked at Lord Durwyn. "Indeed, you are welcome. Clovelly is a lovely village, but did Kenrick warn you that a carriage cannot traverse the streets? They are too narrow and steep. One must walk or ride a donkey down to the Quay."

The viscount smiled. "I think I can manage to make it down to the harbor without fainting or needing to stop and catch my breath."

"Down, yes, but what about back to the top?" Serena asked, hoping to disturb his calm exterior.

The gentleman put his hand to his chest. "Ah, yes, I had forgotten my advanced age."

Jane took the gentleman literally. "We can hire one of the donkeys from Mr. Hannity for you. 'Tis but a half farthing a trip."

Sandy cast his uncle a bold glance. "Why, I shall even provide the fee for the animal myself so as to protect your dignity."

"This very conversation has left my dignity in tatters." The viscount lifted an iris up for inspection, his green eyes twinkling above the purple petals at Serena.

She experienced a strange stirring in the pit of her stomach. It grew harder each day to remember that she wanted him gone. As the others laughed, she noted the look which passed between Sandy and Jane. She returned to her task as the group continued to discuss the village, but her thoughts settled on young Mr. Hart. Here was a young man who was very suited to her cousin. He told them that he only went to London during the Season to please his mother, preferring to stay at the family estate in Surrey. Unfortunately, he was such a gentleman it wasn't likely he would intrude in his uncle's courtship, no matter his obvious attraction for Jane.

Everyone turned at the loud bang of the library door being closed. Mr. Bosworth stepped into the garden. He hurried over to the group and said, "Winslow just informed me that you all are to go to the village church today, and I thought I would accompany you. You ladies will come in the carriage with me and the gentlemen can ride. We shall have nuncheon at the Red Lion."

Durwyn arched one brow as he looked at Serena. "Perchance Mrs. Morgan should like to join us on horseback. I have not forgotten your promise to ride with us."

A flush of pleasure warmed her cheeks that the gentleman had remembered, especially since he had asked her over a week ago. With her uncle going, she didn't need to worry about Jane being left alone in the carriage, so she gave in to her love of riding. "I should be delighted, sir."

Mr. Bosworth made all the arrangements while Serena hurried up to don her maroon riding habit. She lamented the rather faded color and the worn spot where her leg locked through the sidesaddle, but it was the only such riding gown she possessed. Uttering a resigned sigh, she positioned her low crown beaver over her brown curls, then made her way down with the hope that she hadn't kept them waiting.

With the flowers loaded in the family carriage, the party from Bosley Manor set out for the village, which lay south along the coast. Sandy and Kenrick raced ahead of the carriage, leaving Serena and the viscount to canter along some way behind the dust.

Their conversation was restricted to the weather and the countryside for the first few minutes. Then the viscount startled Serena when he asked, "Am I ever to know why you chose to play the highwayman?"

Serena's gaze dropped to her gloved hands, which tightened on the reins. With her uncle's rebukes from last night still very much on her mind, she could only give him a half-truth. "Shall I say that your reputation had preceded you? Jane is no sophisticate who would be able to cope with your dashing lifestyle, sir."

"But Mr. Bosworth doesn't agree with you. His wishes are clear."

"My uncle is much impressed with your station and wealth, sir. He is thinking with a father's pride, which is blinding him to what is truly best for Jane." Serena struggled with how best to explain without betraying what her uncle had forbid her to tell. "Jane is sweet and . . ."

"Extremely naive. But I admire that, Mrs. Morgan. There is nothing more distasteful than a jaded female who is so enamored with Society and all its frivolity that she allows her husband and children to suffer neglect."

"True, but the same could be said of a gentleman whose life is involved with that same frivolity." She stared him straight in the eye.

A dawning look settled on his face. "You feared that I would abandon my wife in the country to pursue my own affairs."

"Has it not been the way you have lived your life?" She drew her gaze back to the carriage, which had drawn to a halt.

"I cannot deny it, ma'am. But has it occurred to you that was because I had no wife and children to watch over? Ask anyone, madam, I am very solicitous of my family. Why, it was family that made me . . ."

The viscount fell silent for a moment and when

he continued, Serena suspected he changed what he had intended to say.

"That is, I well know the worth of my family."

It was strange that he always managed to surprise her. "I am glad to hear that, sir."

Before she had time to ponder the gentleman's words, they arrived to find everyone waiting for them at the carriage park above the town. Clovelly was a quaint fishing village built into the cliffs which overlooked Bideford Bay. The cobblestoned streets descended sharply some four hundred feet toward the bay in a series of terraced steps. Due to the harsh winds which came off the North Atlantic, the village had built a half moon stone quay into the bay, extending from the Red Lion Inn out into the waters. This stone wall formed a calm harbor for the local fishermen to moor their boats.

As the party stood at the top of the village looking down, the London gentlemen were duly impressed. After they had sufficiently admired the view, Serena suggested she would go with the footman to the church and arrange the flowers while the others walked down to the quay. She would join them for nuncheon later.

Mr. Bosworth shook his head. "Kenrick, go with your cousin. It's not as if you haven't been to Clovelly hundreds of times."

For a moment Serena thought her cousin was going to protest. Then he seemed to remember that he needed to earn his father's good opinion. He shrugged and agreed. Lord Durwyn offered his arm to Jane and they headed down the streets, the local citizens calling greetings to Mr. Bosworth's party as they passed.

Serena, sensing Kenrick's impatience, urged him forward as the footman followed behind with the flowers. They made their way through the narrow streets to the chapel, which sat high in the town. She had only just arrived at the church door when the vicar's son, an old friend of Kenrick's, spied his friend from the vicarage porch and called a greeting. Serena, seeing the look on her cousin's face, said, "Go visit with Charles. I don't need help arranging the flowers. I shall come for you when I'm done."

"You are a great gun, Rena." With that, the young man hurried next door.

In the church, she busied herself with the flowers. Within fifteen minutes, she had the lovely blooms settled in two large pewter urns and arranged strategically at the front of the church. Stepping back, she eyed the arrangements with a critical eye and decided they would do. She thanked the footman and went to look for her cousin.

The young man was seated on the front porch of the vicarage with Charles, but they had been joined by several other of Kenrick's local friends, whose names Serena couldn't remember. She signaled to the boy and he rose and took his leave. They made their way to the quay. All the while Kenrick chattered about what his friends had been doing in his absence at school.

Nearing the Red Lion, where the others were awaiting them, Serena caught sight of Mr. Bosworth in deep conversation with Lord Cameron, a local landowner. Fearful what had become of Jane, she searched the waterfront for her cousin. Relief surged in Serena when she spied Jane strolling with Sandy out on the stone quay. Kenrick hurried to join them.

Left alone, Serena wondered what had become of his lordship until she spotted him standing beside a fish vendor near the edge of the harbor. Outrage raced through her as she took in the scene. At the gentleman's side stood Miss Baker, fashionably dressed in a yellow gown with a chip straw bonnet on her fiery red curls. Worse, the chit was hanging on the gentleman's every word as well as his arm. Did he know no shame to be openly flirting right under Jane's and Uncle Gideon's noses?

In the hope of putting an end to the tête-à-tête, Serena approached the couple. Miss Baker looked up and had the decency to blush pink and step away from the viscount. Lord Durwyn turned and smiled, then politely excused himself to his companion

Miss Baker grabbed his arm and drew him down to whisper in his ear.

He patted her hand, but his gaze never left Serena as he replied, "To be sure I will, Miss Baker."

The girl hurried off with only a sullen greeting for Serena as she passed. The viscount came up and smiled. "Mrs. Morgan, would you like to join the others on the seawall?"

She looked over her shoulder at the departing Miss Baker and back to the gentleman. "A tryst, sir? How unwise, with my uncle so near at hand."

His lordship laughed and placed Serena's hand on his arm as he drew her in the direction of the others in their party. "No, my dear madam, a tryst by its very nature must be secret. It was a mere chance encounter." When she cocked one brow in doubt, he added, "If you will remember, it wasn't until this morning that I knew of this planned visit to the village. I see you have much to learn about roguery. But never fear, I'll gladly volunteer to show you all my wicked ways." He waggled his brows at her, a twinkle of pure mischief in his green eyes.

Serena didn't know whether to weep in humiliation at her foolish accusation or laugh at his lighthearted acceptance of her insult. With great effort, she regained her composure and merely said, "Save your wicked ways for London, sir. Ladies in Devonshire prefer honest dealings."

The gentleman halted and turned her to face him. "Do they now, Mrs. Morgan? I have sensed something hidden from us at Bosley Manor since just after our first encounter. You do remember that meeting, do you not, madam? I wonder if the local magistrate would think two masked riders were up to honest dealings?" His gentle smile took the sting out of the accusation.

Her cheeks warmed as she realized the direction her words had taken them. "A mere ploy to protect my cousin from you, sir."

Their gazes locked, and guilt made Serena look away first. But the gentleman gently put his hand to her chin and turned her face back to him. His voice was low and husky. "Do you still think that I would do anything that would hurt that dear sweet child?"

A certainty as she'd never before known came to Serena. No matter his reputation, which seemed to be more rumor than fact, she had found him to be everything a woman could want—handsome, dashing, witty, and, most of all, kind. Everything *she* could want. That thought jarred her. It would never do to fall in love with a man destined for Jane. She breathed deeply to steady her jangled nerves. "No, at least not intentionally."

His hand caressed her chin, and time seemed to stand still. They stood as if trapped in a strange swirl of emotion until the voice of Sir Giles Firth interrupted. "Lord Durwyn! Pray unhand Mrs. Morgan before you set the tongues of this village wagging."

The viscount lowered his hand, but took Serena's and

again drew it through the loop of his arm. "Ah, Sir Miles, is it? What can we do for you?"

The gentleman's face grew mottled with anger. "Giles with a G, sir. You can kindly remember that a lady has a reputation in a small neighborhood that is very fragile." Frustrated by Durwyn's lack of response, the baronet turned his spleen on Serena. "Mrs. Morgan, what can you be thinking to allow this gentleman such liberties? Do you want people to say you are his newest paramour?"

Anger at the baronet overrode any embarrassment she might have ordinarily felt at her situation. "Sir Giles, you overstep your bounds to be reprimanding his lordship or me. Pray forgive us, but I see my uncle signaling us."

"But, madam," he began, then straightened as his gaze moved to where Durwyn had placed a second hand protectively over the gloved one which rested on his arm. "Mrs. Morgan, I beg of you, we must speak in private."

"I cannot at the moment, since we are engaged to dine soon. If you must speak with me, I shall be free in the morning before church. Come to the manor at half past eight. Good day, sir." Serena was relieved when Lord Durwyn drew her away from the irate baronet.

As they made their way to where Mr. Bosworth stood with the others who'd returned from the quay, Serena noted Durwyn's upturned mouth.

"What is there to smile about in that dreadful scene?" she asked.

"Why, only that you now see how easy it is for a rumor to start about someone with only the tiniest bit of truth at its foundation." He squeezed her hand.

Something intense flared inside her. She struggled to

regain her composure and put her mind to the conversation. But the baronet's words replayed in her mind. She and the viscount had done nothing there beside the water. Well, very little. Yet Sir Giles had blown it into a full-fledged affair in a matter of minutes. With dawning realization, she stopped and looked directly into the viscount twinkling eyes. "Lord Durwyn, I do believe I owe you an apology for all the wrong thoughts I've had about you."

"Don't take yourself to task over it, my dear." He leaned close and whispered, "I'll be the first to admit myself no angel. I'm just delighted to discover that you have been thinking of me at all."

Serena blushed, but smiled. "Must we add vanity to your wicked ways?"

"Oh, my dear, I have a variety of failings: impatience, pride, obstinance, vanity." Then he helped her up a set of stairs. "But not sloth. After all, I did walk down here without resorting to the donkeys. Are you not impressed?"

Serena laughed out loud. "Duly impressed, sir." Just then they arrived where the others awaited them, and Mr. Bosworth ushered them into the Red Lion, where he had made arrangements for nuncheon.

As she settled at the table, it occurred to Serena that she'd set out to drive him away and suddenly all she wanted was for him to stay.

Just after eight that evening, Wyn stood at the window in the drawing room, staring into the darkness in thoughtful contemplation. The sound of Miss Bosworth's playing on the pianoforte filled the room behind him as Sandy and the girl's father sat listening. She possessed a bit of talent, which made for a pleasant night's entertainment.

Still, Wyn couldn't deny the evening had been flat for him ever since Mrs. Morgan had said good night and excused herself on matters of household business. His thoughts dwelled on the strange effect the widow had on him. He wanted to know the reason why the woman had fearlessly ridden out to challenge him. It was more than his reputation, he'd stake his life. She had done her best to make his stay uncomfortable, which should have angered him. Yet he'd only seen her as a challenge. It seemed over time he'd discovered her very presence made him enjoy the day.

But she'd avoided him at every turn since their trip to the village. Had he done or said something to upset her? Or was she merely jealous of that simpering Baker chit? He'd seen the look in her lovely eyes as she'd approached them.

Wyn straightened suddenly as a shadowy figure slipped across the terrace and disappeared into the darkness. He recognized the bright green coat and lean frame of young Kenrick Bosworth. What mischief was he up to? The lad had excused himself after they'd dined, claiming he had letters to write about his reinstatement to school, which had greatly pleased his father. Clearly that had been a ruse. Wyn looked back and noted that Mr. Bosworth was sleeping on the sofa while Sandy raptly listened to Jane.

A need to get out of the stuffy room overwhelmed Wyn. He would go out and see what Kenrick was up to and blow a cloud. He moved over to Sandy and whispered in his ear so as not to disturb the young lady's music.

"I just saw young Bosworth slip out, headed toward the cliffs. I think I'll follow and see what he's up to."

Sandy merely nodded his head, never taking his gaze

from Jane. The thought suddenly occurred to Wyn that his nephew was more than a little taken with the girl. What would his mother say to such a marriage? Then it occurred to Wyn that she had described the girl as perfect, so how could she object if Sandy decided to approach Mr. Bosworth to request permission? After all, Wyn had informed him the first night that the girl held no attraction for him.

He put aside his thoughts of Sandy's infatuation. He picked up a candle and lit his cigar, then slipped out the long glass doors into the garden. It took a moment for his eyes to adjust to the darkness. At last he could make out the dark shapes of the shrubs, so he strolled in the direction of the channel. It was a moonless night, but as he drew away from the lights of the manor, he could see well enough to follow the path to the cliffs.

At last he came to the spot where the gravel path turned into stone steps which descended rapidly to the quay that Mr. Bosworth had built. Wyn could just make out the two yachts moored below. Then he caught the flicker of light in the *Little Hawk*. What was Kenrick doing in his father's vessel? In Mr Wyn's presence, Mr. Bosworth had forbidden the boy to take out the boats alone their second day here.

He stood for some minutes smoking. His gaze was riveted on the channel below as he debated whether he should go down. After all, at seventeen the boy might be involved in some romantic assignation. But as that thought occurred, three dark figures stepped from the shadows of the rocks some ten yards down the beach. They moved quickly to the quay and soon boarded the *Little Hawk*.

A worrisome memory filled Wyn as a door opened on the boat and Kenrick appeared in the well-lit portal to welcome his mysterious visitors onboard the yacht. There had been a discussion about smuggling along the north Devon coast at supper one night. Mr. Bosworth had said the tidesmen brought in American tobacco and Irish whiskey on dark nights. Wyn's gaze searched the dark sky, and there wasn't even a sliver of a moon. What better night for such men to ply their trade? And what better adventure for a restless young man to get involved with: something filled with danger that he little understood. And who would take the blame for the boy's misadventure but Serena Morgan? She might be Jane's companion, but it was clear that she had pretty much stepped into the shoes of her dead aunt, caring for both sister and brother.

Without further thought, Wyn ground out his cigar and hurried down the stairs. If the lad was involved in something untoward, Wyn would need to stop him before the yacht could set sail. On reaching the foot of the stairs, he moved noiselessly across the stone quay. The gangway still lay against the quay and Wyn crossed onto the yacht. As he moved along the starboard side of the deck he could hear voices inside. This was no time for polite social graces, so Wyn opened the door and entered without knocking.

Seated round a table with a green baize cloth were Kenrick and three young men of like age. On the table lay four small piles of coins in front of each boy, and young Bosworth was in the process of dealing from a deck of cards. At the sight of the viscount, the young men froze for a moment, then all four jumped to their feet.

"L-Lord Durwyn, would you care to join us?" Kenrick stuttered out the invitation, but it was clear by the fear on his face that he didn't want his lordship there.

Wyn smiled and shook his head. "Be seated gentlemen. I am not in the habit of plucking young men of their allowances." He'd noted the coins were half farthings, which was likely all this lot could afford and wouldn't last long. "I saw the light from the cliffs and wanted to make certain that nothing was happening to your father's vessel. But I see all is well and I interrupted your game, so I shall continue my stroll."

The other lads resettled round the table, but Kenrick nervously fidgeted with the deck. "Do stay and join us after the game when we go to The Salty Sailor's for drinks and something to eat."

"Thank you, no. I prefer to walk." Wyn struggled not to smile at the lad's attempt to sound grown up.

Kenrick bit at his lip, then asked, "You—you won't mention seeing us down here, sir, will you? Papa dislikes gaming excessively."

"I will say nothing to your father." But Wyn knew he must mention what he'd seen to Serena. Likely she could speak with the lad about the evils of gambling without setting his back up. Wyn stepped to the window and drew the curtain shut on the window that had leaked light, then winked at the foursome, who grinned as he exited the cabin.

He moved back onto the stone quay and looked out over the channel for a moment. He could see the lighthouse in the distance on Deadman's Point. Not wanting to return to the manor since Serena had retired for the night, he decided to stroll toward the point instead. He set off along the rocky shore.

Serena sat at the housekeeper's desk going over the weekly accounts. Her household duties were a mere pretext to avoid Lord Durwyn. The truth was she needed to put some distance between herself and the viscount. He was proving to be too much of a distraction for her.

"Is there a problem, Mrs. Morgan?" The housekeeper eyed her mistress with concern. She had been a loyal servant to the Bosworth family for over ten years, and this unexpected visit late on Saturday night had ruffled her feathers.

"Oh, no, Mrs. Ridley. The accounts are in order as always." Serena smiled reassuringly at the woman.

"Will you be joining the others for tea, madam?"

Temptation to spend the evening in the viscount's company beckoned, but Serena decided she would be better served going to her room. "I think not. If you will prepare a tray for two, I shall join Kenrick in the library."

"Very good, ma'am." The housekeeper departed. Minutes later, Caleb the underfootman appeared at the doorway.

Serena led him to the library, where she tapped softly. There was no answer, so she opened the door and found the room empty. "Put the tea tray on the table"—she gestured to a small table near the window— "and go see if Mr. Kenrick is in his room, Caleb. Ask him to join me here."

Still unconcerned, Serena poured out two cups of tea and added milk and sugar the way her cousin liked. She sat down to await the lad and nibbled on an almond biscuit as she stared out at the channel. She wondered how much longer the viscount would be their guest. It was plain to her that Jane, while she enjoyed the gentleman's gentle teasing, showed no decided preference for Lord Durwyn. In fact, she seemed much more drawn to the one closest to her in age, Mr. Hart. It was a shame that Uncle Gideon was so set on the viscount for his daughter.

"Ma'am." The footman stood in the doorway, taking a moment to catch his breath. "Mr. Kenrick don't appear to be in the manor."

Alarm raced through Serena. "Are you certain, Caleb? He said he was going to write some letters."

"There's ink and paper on his desk, ma'am, but he ain't there. So I went to the drawin' room to see if he'd joined the others, and Mr. Hart informed me that the viscount went down to the cove after Mr. Kenrick."

Serena struggled to keep her voice even. Had the two of them slipped away for some mischief? Then she vaguely remembered a discussion of sailing at nuncheon that day. Is that what they were about? Seeing the footman staring at her, she gathered her wits and said, "Thank you, Caleb, that will be all this evening."

The servant bowed and closed the door, leaving Serena alone. She was so upset she wanted to toss her cup against the wall. In her anger she spoke out loud to herself. "If he has convinced that foolish Kenrick to go sailing tonight, I shall . . . I shall . . ." She didn't know what she would do or say, but whatever it was it would be in a very loud voice. Without a word to anyone, she went to her room to retrieve her shawl, then set out for the shore in search of Lord Durwyn and her cousin, hopefully before they embarked on their little adventure.

Chapter Four

A gentle wind tugged at Serena's skirts as she stood at the top of the cliff that overlooked Bristol Channel. Her uncle's newly built quay lay in darkness, but she could make out the tall spires of both yachts against the night sky still in their moorings. When she saw the faint glimmer of light coming from the *Little Hawk,* a sense of relief raced through her that she had caught them before they set sail.

She hastened down the steps and onto the quay. The water was just rough enough to make her take caution as she mounted the gangway to the yacht. At last she reached the cabin door and stepped into the small room. A lone candle burned on a table.

"Kenrick," she called, but received no response, either inside or out. No one was there, but they had been. The viscount's scent of sandalwood still lingered in the enclosed cabin.

Serena blew out the candle and stepped on the deck to ponder where her cousin and the viscount might have gone. She peered down the narrow arch of sand to the south. A chilling sensation overcame her. She had long known that these beaches were active with smugglers. Men who were utterly dangerous and ruthless. She had often warned Kenrick to avoid them. Surely his lordship wouldn't have gotten involved in trying to meet such men. But she reminded herself he hadn't gotten a reputation as a rogue by sitting in his room at night.

She quickly dismissed such an idea, but another possibility soon replaced the first one. She gasped. Was the viscount involved in a tryst? She had just assumed that the viscount and her cousin were together, but Durwyn had gone out after Kenrick.

The memory of Miss Baker whispering in his ear that afternoon returned to her. What was it he had replied? "To be sure I will." Had he had the audacity to arrange a dalliance right in front of her? Was he showing her more of his wicked ways? A wave of suspicion came over her, and she suddenly wanted to know the truth.

She climbed back ashore and turned to survey the narrow shoreline. There seemed to be nothing moving but the steady roll of the incoming waves. As she looked south, she caught the glint of the lighthouse at Deadman's Point. What a perfect place to arrange a clandestine meet. Mr. Wimberly, the old lighthouse keeper, was practically deaf. Once he lit the light at night and went to bed, he would never know he'd had late night visitors.

Driven by a strange need to know, Serena set off down the beach toward the soft glow. Yet somehow she couldn't fully explain to herself why she was so determined to find Lord Durwyn. Her primary concern should have been Kenrick. But her cousin had never before been foolish enough to brave the beaches at night. He'd always had a healthy respect for the danger of the Free Traders.

Lost in her thoughts, Serena didn't hear the rapid approach of footsteps from the shadows of a small cove. Suddenly a hand clamped over her mouth and she found herself lifted off the ground. She struggled with all her might, but to no avail. Her captor proved too strong.

He hauled her, kicking and trying to scream past the hands that restrained her, into one of the many small caves dotting the beach. Her foot struck his shin and a notable groan emanated from him before he whispered, "Be quiet, and do stop kicking. It's me, Serena."

She relaxed the moment she recognized the viscount's voice. A thrill filled her to hear her Christian name on his lips. He dropped his hand from her mouth and turned her to face him. "Are you all right? I didn't hurt you, did I?"

She was strangely aware that he held her in his arms and that she felt safe. "What are you doing here?"

"Shhhhhh! This cave will make our voices echo on the beach. There are several of The Gentlemen unloading a boat beyond the next stand of rocks," he whispered.

She couldn't see his face, but the whisper of his breath against her cheek sent a tremor through her. His hands slid down her arms. Then he released her and stepped away.

Disappointment welled up. Then she reminded herself of her responsibilities. "Where is Kenrick?" She'd lowered her voice to match his.

"He and his friends were on the *Little Hawk,* playing whist when I came past. If they are gone, no doubt, one of them is in possession of the others' quarterly allowances. I would guess they have gone off to The Salty Sailor for a few revels." He moved to position himself protectively between her and the opening of the cave.

A sense of relief made her sag back against the cold rock of the curved wall. She peered out into the night, but could see nothing but the roiling movement of the seas. The sounds of the waves lapping at the nearby rocks rang in the small space, but despite their danger of discovery it was surprisingly soothing to one's nerves. Yet the stone walls and the dampness of the cave made her shudder. She wrapped her arms about her to ward off the chill.

"How long must we stay here?"

Durwyn slid his arm round her shoulders in an unobtrusive manner to warm her. "Not long, I'm sure. Those fellows won't want to linger on the beach for long. Don't be afraid."

He smelled enticingly of cigars and sandalwood. She resisted the improper urge to lean into the sensual warmth of him. In her few years as a young bride, she'd never known this urge to press herself against her husband, to wish for a kiss or a caress.

She forced herself not to think about what it would be like with the viscount, instead trying to make reasonable conversation. "Oh, there is nothing to fear as long as we stay out of their way. True fear is when the wagon you are riding in gets cut off by a band of French marauders looking for food and they shoot the driver."

"Ah, yes, your life following the drum. What did you do?"

Serena could hear the interest in his voice. "What else could I do but climb into the seat and spring the team? None of the other females had ever tooled so much as a gig."

He chuckled. "May I say I'm not surprised, but I would guess your Frenchmen were?"

She smiled at his praise. "By the time they realized what was happening, I had left them in our dust. Several of the officers heard the women's cries and came to our rescue. In truth it was over in a matter of ten minutes, but it was the longest ten minutes of my life."

He began to ask her questions about her life in Portugal, and she told stories that she had never told even her family. Somehow it didn't seem right to frighten Jane with the ugliness or romanticize war for Kenrick.

Wyn listened to her tales of life as an Army wife. Major Morgan had been one of those men who wanted her with him despite the danger to her. Wyn suspected that the life had been far more difficult than she was telling. She had suffered all that and lost her husband as well. A surge of protectiveness rose in him and he wanted to draw her into his arms and tell her she would never have to face such hardships again. But who was he to be saying such to her?

Suddenly curiosity and an unreasonable twinge of jealousy got the better of him. "I hope you don't mind my being personal, but do you miss the major a great deal?"

In the dim light of the cave, he saw her bow her head, and he cursed himself for his unthinking question. No doubt she still grieved for the man. Then, to his surprise, she spoke in a clear, unemotional voice.

"While the marriage wasn't a love match, my husband was a good man." She was silent a moment, then added, "I cannot deny that I miss the life of adventure he brought to me, but he was rather too duty bound to make a good husband. I think he valued my nursing talents far more than any other skill I brought to him."

Adventure? Wyn thought that an odd thing for a woman to miss about her marriage. Then it dawned on him. She had never known true love or passion. He experienced a sudden raw need to claim her as his own.

He wanted to be the one to make her weak with desire and breathless for his kisses.

"Serena!" He whispered her name, then tilted her chin up and kissed her. Without hesitation she surrendered herself into his arms. The fire ignited between them and flamed to an intensity that surprised even Wyn. In a flash, their passion was doused by a wave from the incoming tide which rolled into the cave and soaked their feet.

Brought back to reality by the cold water, Wyn grabbed Serena's hand and pulled her toward the cave opening. "Hurry or we'll be trapped here by high tide."

Outside, there was no visible stretch of sand in either direction. The sea had come in and waves splashed against the rocky cliff. "We're trapped. Can you climb?"

"Yes." There was no hesitation in her voice.

Wyn lifted her onto a nearby boulder, then watched as she started the difficult climb up the side of the cliff. He couldn't help but admire her pluck. As a wave splashed at his knee, he scrambled up the rocks behind her. Some ten feet up the path, she slipped and slid halfway back to him, and his heart plummeted. He reached out and grabbed for her but she came to rest just short of him.

"Are you all right? Can I help you?" The thought that she might fall and be killed twisted in his gut. As if someone had just fired a gun, Wyn knew he didn't just desire her, he loved her. He couldn't think straight when he thought of her hurt or dead. This climb in the dark was too dangerous. "Perhaps we should wait out the tide here?"

"It's just loose rock. I was going too fast. I can make it." She stood, leaning into the side of the cliff. She began to slowly pick her way up the hillside.

Wyn moved closer behind her, but this time her footing was more secure. It took close to thirty minutes for them to scale the incline. At last they made it to the top. He took her in his arms and hugged her to him. "Are you unhurt, my dear?"

A voice echoed in the distance. "Lord Durwyn? Serena?" The viscount recognized Mr. Bosworth's voice.

The widow started and drew back from Wyn's embrace. "Here, Uncle."

"Serena, I want—" Wyn began, hoping to tell her of his love, but she held up her hand to silence him as the older gentleman appeared out of the darkness.

"Serena," Mr. Bosworth snapped, "what are you doing out here? Mr. Hart told me that it was Kenrick who was out here with the viscount. Then Kenrick arrived back from the inn to say that he'd inquired for you, only to find you'd gone out."

"I followed the men. I was looking for Kenrick, sir."

Wyn interceded. "Sir, Mrs. Morgan and I met on the beach. Then the tide caught us. We were forced to climb, and I fear our feet are wet. We should get your niece out of this wind, and I own I should like to change my clothes as well."

The old gentleman looked from Serena to the viscount. It was clear he had questions, but he held his tongue. "Very well, it's late."

They had a silent trip back to the manor. Unfortunately, Wyn never got a chance to speak with Serena alone before her uncle ordered her upstairs to bed.

The lady had scarcely disappeared when Mr. Bosworth said, "I think you and I should meet in the morning, sir. There are things we should discuss. My library at seven sharp."

Wyn's first thought was to try and explain about their escapade tonight, but then he thought there was no point. He would inform the gentleman in the morning that he had no intention of offering for Jane. "I shall be there, sir."

He bid the gentleman good night, then went up to Sandy's room and knocked. The lad appeared in his shirtsleeves. "Where have you been, Uncle?"

"I shall tell you at breakfast. I wanted you to know that I shall meet with Bosworth at eight in the morning."

Sandy's face blanched white. "But—but you said—"

A smile tipped Wyn's mouth. "Never fear, lad, I'm asking to pay my addresses to the lovely widow. If you've something to ask the old gentleman, be up and ready to speak your piece."

The young man eyed his uncle curiously. "You've no objection, sir?"

"None whatsoever, but don't you think you should speak to your parents first? It's rather an important decision, and they might object."

The young man's chin came up. "I've my grandmother's estate and a modest income. I shall make my own choice in this matter, sir."

Wyn's smile widened. "Good luck, then." As he made his way to his room, he thought that Sandy had found independence from his parents in his desire to wed Miss Bosworth. The boy . . . he paused at that word, then grinned to himself. No, Sandy was now a young man. He would do well on his own.

But what about Serena? Did she love Durwyn? The memory of that kiss in the cave bolstered his confidence as he entered his room for the night.

Serena overslept the following morning. Guilt at her conduct in the cave had kept her tossing and turning until the wee hours. She had fallen in love with the man who was intended for Jane. Worse, she didn't even know if he loved her or found her an amusing dalliance—but she wouldn't entertain that idea about the gentleman. Jane's welfare and happiness came first.

It was nearing a quarter past eight as she came down the stairs to the great hall. As she moved past the library, she heard the murmur of voices and halted. She looked over her shoulder to see one of the maids putting fresh flowers in a vase.

"Mary, who is in the library?"

The girl bobbed a curtsy. "I don't rightly know, ma'am. Mr. Bosworth and Lord Durwyn went in early this morning, but I'm not certain if it still be the gentlemen."

Serena's heart plummeted. So by morning's end, she might have to face the man she loved and watch as he announced his engagement to Jane. Her back stiffened, and she promised herself she wouldn't wear her heart on her sleeve. She couldn't ask for more for her dear sweet cousin, but why did it have to hurt so very much?

At that moment the knocker sounded on the front door. A footman hurried to answer the summons. The door opened to reveal Sir Giles Firth, looking as if he'd sucked on a lemon for much of the morning. He marched into the hall and announced, "I have an appointment with Mrs. Morgan."

Serena didn't think her heart could sink much lower, but the sight of the gentleman left her utterly dismal. She would now have to face the haranguing of the baronet about her conduct in Clovelly.

The library door opened before she could greet her caller. Mr. Bosworth stepped out and called, "Jamie, bring champagne." He spied his niece. "Ah, my dear, come join the celebration."

She looked from her uncle to Sir Giles, who was rapidly moving across the floor to where she stood. "Mrs. Morgan, I must have a word with you."

The urge to turn on her heel and run came to Serena, but she'd never backed down from a difficult task. Before she could make up her mind which torture she would face first, Lord Durwyn came out the library door. In an instant he took in the advancing baronet and he moved to take a startled Serena in his arms.

"My dear beautiful Rena." To the amazement of the maid, the footman, and the other two gentlemen, the viscount lowered his head and soundly kissed the lady, who didn't object in the least.

"Unhand that woman, sir," Sir Giles barked, his face flushing quite red. "Mr. Bosworth, don't just stand there. Help the lady."

Mr. Bosworth eyed the kissing pair and shrugged. "She's a grown woman, sir. If she wants to kiss the viscount, I've no say in the matter."

The baronet moved closer to the embracing couple. "Mrs. Morgan!"

Yet the two seemed unaware of anything and anyone in the room. At last Wyn drew back and looked into the bemused face of Serena. "Rena, forgive my boldness, but after all I am a rogue." He grinned at her a moment then grew serious. "I could not wait to tell you I love you."

"Lord Durwyn!" Sir Giles snapped.

Serena blinked up into Wyn's handsome face, a range of emotions flitting across her countenance, the final one despair. She turned to her uncle, who smiled his approval. Worrying her lip, she returned her gaze to the man who held her tightly. "W-what about Jane?"

"Mrs. Morgan!" Sir Giles tried again, his tone growing louder.

The viscount lifted a hand up to caress her face, never taking his eyes from hers. "Sandy summoned her down earlier and is asking for her hand in the garden as we speak. I wish to do the same to you, dear heart."

"Sir," the baronet barked, "I won't be ignored."

Serena, paying no heed to the man beside them, cast a questioning glance at her uncle. He nodded his head. "I've told them everything my dear. I could do nothing less." A smile brightened the old gentleman's face. "Young Mr. Hart said he didn't care, he would protect and love her until his last breath." Mr. Bosworth brushed away tears of happiness. "I can ask for no more from the lad."

Serena peered guiltily at the man she loved. "Now you know. Can you forgive us?"

Wyn drew her tighter into his arms. "There is nothing to forgive. She is a beautiful, sweet child who will love Sandy as he deserves. You did what was best for Jane." Seeing the relief and joy on the lady's face, he said, "What I wish to ask is will you marry me, dear heart?"

"Madam, heed me." Sir Giles roared, but before he could say more, Mr. Bosworth stepped up and clamped a hand on the man's shoulder.

"Enough of this nonsense, man. Can you not see you are interrupting a private moment?"

"But—but . . ." Sir Giles looked from Mrs. Morgan to Lord Durwyn and saw such profound emotion he seemed embarrassed. He shook off the old man's hand. "It seems I was greatly mistaken in Mrs. Morgan's character."

Lord Durwyn picked that moment to heed the man's words. His hand shot out to clutch the baronet's lapel. Wyn's stare was frigid. "Is there something you wished to say about my future wife?"

Sir Giles visibly quaked. He tugged at the gentleman's hand, then fell back when the viscount released him.

"N-no, I was just leaving, sir." He hurried to the door, then looked back from the wider distance. "M-may I wish you happy?" With that he slipped from the manor.

The viscount arched one eye brow. "I thought he'd never leave." He drew Serena back into the circle of his arms.

Mr. Bosworth looked at the couple and a dawning look came to his face. "Pray forgive me, but I must see how Jane and her young man are doing." He left Serena and Wyn alone.

Wyn held his love at arm's length. "Can you ever forgive me for such a display of affection in front of others? I couldn't wait and allow Sir Giles to ask you first."

Serena laughed. "He was more likely to read me a lecture than ask for my hand, sir."

"Oh, I think he thought he would be rescuing you from my raffish clutches." He slid his arms round her, then leaned down and kissed her.

She sighed contentedly. "It's plain to see he doesn't know what a woman wants."

"And what does this woman want?" He eyed her hungrily.

"To be yours forever."

That was exactly what the viscount wanted to hear, and he showed her just how happy she'd made him.

June arrived in London with no word from Lord Durwyn or Sandy. Lady Hartford and her sisters were at the their weekly tea, but her ladyship's composure showed cracks. Instead of overseeing her tea party with her usual grand style, she paced nervously about the room.

"I've heard nothing from Alexander since the letter I received just after they arrived at Bosley Manor. What can Durwyn be doing? He has never been so slow about matters. Do you think something is wrong?"

Sophia and Elyse exchanged a look before the younger said, "Likely he's up to his old antics. Remember, my dear, we forced him to go to meet your young lady. For all we know, he took her in dislike and the gentlemen have gone off on some new adventure. He's not likely to write and tell you that he has disregarded our wishes."

The baroness harrumphed. "My son will live to rue the day if he has—" The lady paused as her butler opened the drawing room door.

"Yes, Asher."

The old gentleman stood formally and announced, "Lord and Lady Durwyn, madam."

A large smile bloomed on Lady Hartford and to her sisters she boasted, "I knew how it would be. We have done well, sisters."

All eyes were on the door, through which passed Viscount Durwyn with a young lady the baroness vaguely remembered. Where had she seen her before? The lady was fashionably dressed in a dark green striped gown and lovely bonnet. Then the baroness's eyes widened as she remembered this was Miss Bosworth's companion, and a widow to boot. Why, she hadn't a feather to fly with. What foolish thing had her brother done? Her mouth fell open at the passionate look that passed between the newlyweds. Still reeling from the shock, the lady was little prepared for the second set of names that came from the butler.

"Mr. and Mrs. Alexander Hart and Mr. Bosworth."

Lady Hartford sat down hard. Alexander married? Her gaze locked on the door, and she gasped when her son led Jane Bosworth, breathtaking in a fashionable blue muslin gown with embroidered yellow flowers at the hem, into the drawing room. Her son looked supremely happy and quite grown up as he masterfully led Jane to a chair, then directed his father-in-law to a chair while he greeted his aunts.

Lord Durwyn called, "Good morning, dear sisters. I see our timing is superb and that we have found you together. May I present my wife, Serena, Lady Durwyn, as well as Sandy's wife, Jane, Mrs. Hart, and of course, Mr. Bosworth."

At last finding her tongue, the baroness sputtered, "What is the meaning of this, sir? My son married?"

To everyone's amazement, young Sandy gamely said, "I am, Mother, and I'll tolerate no censure." He looked at Jane with such adoration that there could be little doubt that he loved his new bride. "I'm hoping you will welcome Jane to our family."

Lady Hartford started to her feet. "If you think I shall not have my say—"

The viscount was at her side immediately. "Cat, I would have a word with you in the library." Seeing the imminent refusal on her face, he snapped, "Now." He looked up to see a determined Sandy advancing on his mother and held up his hand. "I shall handle this dear boy. See to your wife and father-in-law."

Sandy halted and looked back at Jane, whose eyes had grown wide and terrified. He immediately returned to her side and whispered into her ear. She took his hand and a serene calm came over her. She gave him a trusting smile.

The viscount escorted his sister to the door, but called over his shoulder, "Elyse, would you act as hostess while Cat and I discuss this matter? I'm sure everyone could use a refreshing cup of tea."

Moments later, Wyn closed the door to the library. "Catherine, do not do anything that you might regret."

"How dare you criticize my handling of my son! How could you allow Alexander to throw himself away on that girl? I had the Marquess of Andover's daughter in mind for him." She put her arms akimbo on her ample hips.

The viscount crossed his arms over his chest. "You thought Jane perfect a scant two months ago."

"For you, not my son."

He eyed his sister thoughtfully. Deep down she loved her son and eventually would come to love Jane if she got the chance. He didn't want her temper to put a wall between herself and the young couple that would take years to break down. "Catherine, sit down. There is something I must tell you."

A frightened expression came on her ladyship's face, but she did as she was bade. Wyn quickly sketched out Jane's history and her disability. "Cat, Sandy loves this girl with all his heart. In most ways she can live the perfect life of wife and mother. She is sweetly innocent and takes most people at face value. But she has no mother to guide her through the rocky shoals of Society. Can you not get past your anger and embrace this young woman, who loves Sandy? I'm certain Mr. Bosworth would welcome your support for his only daughter."

A dawning look came on the lady's face. She rose and straightened, then reached a hand out and grabbed her brother's hand. "Thank you for keeping me from being an utter fool. Why, that dear girl can count on me to guide her through this difficult time. I must go. My guests are waiting."

She hurried from the room, and Wyn followed in her wake. He stood in the doorway and watched as she went to welcome her new daughter-in-law with a kiss, then embrace her son and praise his beautiful wife. It was as if a different woman had returned from the one who'd left.

Serena came to where her husband stood. Wyn drew her across the hall to the library and closed the door.

"What did you do to wreak such a change in your sister?" she asked as he drew her into his arms.

"I told her she had the perfect wife for Sandy—a beautiful young lady of wealth and genteel family who will welcome her help and, more importantly, her advice as no other lady of the *ton* would. What mother-in-law can resist a new daughter-in-law who will heed her words of wisdom and advice? So you need no longer worry about our Jane." He kissed away the frown on his wife's forehead.

"I shall always worry about her, but much less so now that I know she has someone like Sandy to love and protect her as she deserves." She reserved judgment on Lady Hartford for the moment, but there was little doubt that Jane could charm even her with her sweet innocence.

"As do you, my lovely." He tightened his hold and she rested her head on his shoulder. They both enjoyed the simple intimacy of just being in one another's arms.

Serena lifted her head from his shoulder and arched a brow. "Protected by a rogue? Is that not rather like setting the fox to watch the henhouse?"

He brushed a wispy brown curl from her brow. "Perhaps. Only remember that you shall have a lifetime to reform me, my love."

Her eyes twinkled. "I'm not sure I want you to forget *all* your wicked ways."

He waggled his brows wickedly. "Then I shall have

to show them to you one by one. Shall we begin?" He lowered his lips to hers. For just the briefest of moments, Serena was certain she would always love her rogue, reformed or not. Then all thoughts were swept away on a tide of consuming emotions.

THE TABLES TURNED

Victoria Hinshaw

Chapter One

Lord Daniel Dashworth's brain was afire in his pounding skull. Every jostling step of his horse rattled his aching bones and roiled his sour stomach as they plodded along the deserted road. The day lacked only a howling hailstorm to be the most disagreeable of his entire twenty-nine years.

Dash owed his extreme discomfort to his stubborn refusal to postpone the boast he made last night. Whatever had possessed him to declare to his friends that he would set out the following day on a wilderness adventure, with only his horse as company? Actually he knew precisely why he made that skitter-witted pledge. The culprit was a commendable vintage, an exceptional barrel, but multiple bottles. Many multiples.

So while his friends snored away this morning, he had staggered to the stable and somehow mounted Ajax. His valet, Mullins, ever obedient, had awakened, shaved and dressed him, and even helped to saddle the horse. Now Dash was finally out of the environs of his hunting box, far enough away to stop before his head split wide open or he cast up his accounts. Or both.

At the village just ahead there was a small inn, good enough for a brief respite from his agony. The four of them must have emptied more than a dozen bottles last night. And all he could remember after his glib pledge was the wager the other three made on his success in evading Society for six weeks.

He sat his horse miserably. If any of the blades who made up his group saw him slumped in the saddle, they would make his anguish the butt of their laughter for years to come, tell the story over and over to any who would listen. *So does the noble Lord Daniel ride off on his crusade to find a purpose for his dreary life.*

What the devil had he been thinking of to ask such pointless questions of himself last night? No one ever cared what happened to the second son of a duke, as long as the fellow stood by until the heir had a son of his own. That had always sufficed as the purpose for his life. Friendly drinking, a comely mistress, a bit of sport here and there made a fine existence. Why now, at the cusp of his third decade, did he get the mad notion he needed some other raison d'être?

A wilderness experience to refresh his spirit? Humbug!

He took a few swallows from the wineskin hanging from his saddle. Ah, the noble Mullins. He always knew what was best for his master. Too bad the master was the veriest nodcock.

To entertain himself and divert his mind from his own stupidity, he began to sing out loud, though both the melody and the words were foggy in his head. "'Sometime in the month of June, when I did something with a spoon . . .'"

Miss Anne Talcott pulled her dark cloak close about her and strode through the wood beyond the inn's stableyard. She needed a reviving walk and a few breaths of fresh air after sitting at Mary's side the entire clock around, sponging the maid's forehead and arms, and listening to her moans in the overheated room.

The Lamb and Lark was not much of a hostelry, but as its only current patron, she found it reasonably satisfactory. Only because one of her grooms had grown up nearby had they been able to turn off the main road and find accommodations quickly enough to put Mary, Anne's maid, to bed before she suffered the worst effects of her putrid throat and wretched chills.

Poor Mary. She was quite distraught at putting her mistress to such bother. Now that the maid felt a little better and had taken a few spoonfuls of gruel, Anne decided she could leave her in the care of the innkeeper's daughter for an hour. She had peeked into the stable to see her grooms playing dice, and without them noticing her, she hurried away and whistled softly to Ursa, now off following his own paths through the woods.

The day was crisp, the spring air clear, the sun bright in the sky. The birds' calls, the rustle of the leaves beneath her feet, the music of the countryside surrounded her. It felt good to be out of doors, and not sitting in a hot room or a bumpy coach, even if she was sorry her arrival in London would be postponed a few days.

"'. . . In 'is hand a jug o' punch . . .'"

Anne stopped and listened. An off-key voice came closer. She saw the road ahead between the trees and walked toward it.

"'. . . And on 'is knee a pretty wench . . .'"

Who would be singing drunken ditties two hours before noontide?

"'Deedle, deedle, dum, dum . . .'"

The horseman who came into view was draped over his horse, hardly a proper seat. The beast, head hanging

low, walked slowly, as one entirely committed to endur-
ing patiently the most egregious behavior of its rider.

"' . . . And on his knee a pretty wench . . .'"

"Sir! Sir!" Anne called out in her most commanding
voice.

"Whoa, Ajax." The rider raised his head and squinted
in her direction. "Who's there?"

Anne marched toward the horse, leaving the trees behind her. "Sir, you are disturbing the peace of this
woods and may soon offend the ears of the good women
and children of Stoneby, the village you are about to
enter."

As she spoke, Anne assessed the man's condition. His
coat was well-tailored and his cravat clean, though disheveled. He looked to be well into his cups so early in
the day.

He leaned toward her, almost lost his balance, and
swung himself back just in time. "Who are you?"

"One who has had her peaceful contemplation of the
local verdure interrupted in a most jarring way."

"Well, Mother, I 'pectfully beg your pardon, but all
that stops the anvil clanging in my brainbox is my
song—"

"Mother? Whatever do you . . ." Anne swallowed the
rest of her words. Of course, with her hair sleeked back
in a bun and her shoulders wrapped in this heavy cloak,
he thought her an old woman of the village. "Nevertheless, I ask that you please desist making that racket
before every person in the village disrupts his labor to
see what creature is being skinned alive."

He tilted towards her again, then lurched backward,
barely keeping his seat.

"Now I see you're not so old. What are you doing
here alone on this road?"

"A mere handful of steps from the inn, sir. And I am not alone." She gave a little whistle and Ursa trotted up beside her almost immediately.

"The devil!" The rider rubbed his eyes.

"No, just my companion Ursa." No one would dare come near her when the huge black Newfoundland was present.

The rider began to laugh and, reins slack, dropped his head onto his mount's neck again. The horse took up his careless amble once more. Within a few paces, the rider sang out again, to no particular tune, "'A jug o' punch, a tidy wench, diddle diddle dum . . .'"

Anne nearly sputtered with rage at his cavalier behavior. Though he was dressed as a gentleman, his manners were deplorable, his singing execrable, the song inappropriate for the ears of children. Or respectable persons of any age!

What a thoroughly wicked individual. She was quite sorry she had even attempted to address the wretch.

She spun around and tramped back to the woodland path. The innkeeper said this trail led to a pretty stream with a little waterfall. Heavens above, now she needed a few moments of tranquillity even more!

Dash awoke to the tantalizing aroma of roasting mutton, a smell that reminded each fiber of his being how many hours had passed since its last nourishment. He rolled out of bed and tried to still the throbbing in his head. Without a servant at hand, he had no choice but to descend the stairs himself if he wanted a tankard of ale and a slice of that roast. Someone had brought his small valise upstairs and must have helped him off with his jacket. He had little memory of his arrival, except that a sturdy coach stood in the yard and a team of horses chomped away in the stable when he took Ajax into a stall.

The rest was a blur.

Except that crazy woman who had hollered at him just before he arrived.

He splashed water on his face, brushed his teeth, and peered into the mirror in order to comb his hair. His neckcloth was limp and drooping, but otherwise he thought he looked remarkably well for a man whose head felt like its circumference had grown to ten or twelve feet.

Slowly he tiptoed down the staircase and followed the richly mouthwatering scents of a grand English mutton dinner. Dash knew not which was worse, the grumbling in his stomach or the thudding in his head. He paused in the entrance to the taproom. One figure occupied one table in the small chamber, a lady with her back to him. Two hulking fellows he thought might be the grooms he had seen earlier sat near the fire, each with a mug in his hand.

The dog lay by the fire, a large bone near its head. When Dash walked into the room, it snapped to attention and growled.

The men looked up and the lady turned around to look at him. With a sinking heart, Dash realized she was his tormentor from the morning. "Excuse me, is the proprietor on hand?"

"Shush, Ursa! Stay." She watched the dog settle back to the floor, then spoke again. "Mr. Hitchcock is in the pantry."

He walked into room and faced the lady. "I am Daniel Dashworth, at your service."

She frowned and nodded, looking stern. "Yes, Mr.

Hitchcock told us of your arrival." She looked away and took another bite of her meal.

"I see." He stood awkwardly, shifting from one foot to the other for what seemed an eternity before Mr. Hitchcock came back.

"Ah, m'lord, be ye wantin' some dinner?"

"If you please. And an ale. And may I inquire if you might have a headache powder on hand?"

Before the innkeeper answered, the lady spoke again. "I anticipated you might be in need of such a remedy. Here is a large dose for you." She took a folded paper out of her reticule and held it out.

He stepped closer and took it. "Thank you, madam. I am surely in your debt. Also for spoiling your morning walk."

"I am Miss Talcott, Miss Anne Talcott of Dalby."

"Beggin' yer pardon, miss. There's no fire lit in the other parlor. Do ye mind if I seat Lord Daniel in here?"

"I would be most uncharitable if I forced Lord Daniel to a chilly parlor, Mr. Hitchcock."

Dash bowed, once again painfully jostling the contents of his skull. "Thank you, Miss Talcott. I appreciate your generosity."

She gave a half snicker, half sniff, quickly smothered in her napkin. "Please be seated, Lord Daniel."

Hitchcock scurried to the barrel and began to draw a tankard of ale.

Dash took a chair at the table next to hers. "I wish to apologize for my disgraceful behavior earlier. I admit to having had more to drink than usual, a very embarrassing situation."

"So I would imagine." Her gaze concentrated on her plate as she speared a piece of mutton.

The innkeeper set the tankard and a small glass in front of Dash. "I'll get yer dinner, milord."

Dash emptied the paper of headache powder into his glass, added a splash of ale and swirled it for a moment before he downed the concoction.

"I feel better already. You see, Miss Talcott, I was the unwitting victim of my friends' exuberance. They were attempting to celebrate my natal day and their efforts got a bit out of hand." Why he felt he had to explain, Dash could not fathom. It simply seemed necessary, though he discreetly omitted the parts about the presence of the muslin set and how he had sent Camilla on her way back to London with a handsome bauble.

Miss Talcott chewed, looking unimpressed. With the brighter light falling on her face, Dash noticed she was considerably younger than he had thought. Despite her severely drawn back hair and drab, high-necked gown, she looked barely out of the schoolroom, with smooth cheeks, delicately formed pink lips, and large gray eyes fringed with thick lashes.

She swallowed and gazed at him, raising her brows. "May I offer my felicitations on your birthday, my lord?"

He detected a touch of teasing in her words. "I accept your offer with gratitude. May I ask what brings you to this, ah, rather remote village, Miss Talcott?" He tried his most appealing smile, headache be damned.

"My maid took ill on our journey to London and we turned off the main road to find a quiet place for her to recuperate for a day or two."

Abruptly he heard the dog loudly crunch its bone, noisily grinding it to bits. The animal's dark brown eyes seemed glued to Dash's ankles.

Mr. Hitchcock set down a large plate of mutton,

potatoes, and carrots, crowned with a huge hunk of bread. The aroma was intoxicating, and Dash forced himself not to scoop the food into his mouth as fast as he could. He picked up a forkful and gave a sigh of satisfaction as the flavor of the meat met his tongue.

She spoke in a near whisper. "This inn is small and hardly luxurious, but I have found Mrs. Hitchcock's cooking a delightful surprise."

"Mmmmm." He hoped his response was adequate.

She pushed her plate away from the edge of the table. "And the portions are huge."

The dog slurped its tongue across its lips. Dash refused to look in its direction.

He put down his fork for a moment. "Why are you going to London, Miss Talcott?"

"I will join my father, Baron Talcott of Dalby, who has been in town since January."

"If, perhaps, you attend some of the activities of the *ton*, I might encounter you in London." What was he saying? He was supposed to be heading off to the wilderness.

"I doubt I shall be going to many routs. And I plan to spend some time with my cousin Sarah, Lady Easterly, who lost her husband a year ago. I am looking forward to visiting the sights, listening to the lectures of the Royal Society, and perhaps seeing the plays of Shakespeare."

Ah, Dash thought, a bluestocking. "London has attractions to delight the senses of all sorts of people. What activities do you consider fun, Miss Talcott?"

"My pleasures are quite rural in nature, Lord Daniel. I enjoy a walk along the fields at sunrise, a ride through hills on my mare." She had a thoughtful look, staring into the distance. "Visiting the needy and the sick gives me more satisfaction than it should. I reproach myself for gaining more contentment from my charitable efforts than the small comforts give to those I try to benefit."

Not only a bluestocking, Dash thought, but one of those self-righteous do-gooders as well. "How very virtuous of you."

"What do you do for enjoyment, Lord Daniel?"

"Oh, I try to enjoy everything I do." *And those activities are hardly suited for your ears, my dear.* "I have, ah . . . you see . . ."

What did he do for pure fun? At the moment, nothing in particular occurred to him. How odd. "Yes, as I say, I try to do everything for pleasure, for what other reason could there be but one's own gratification for rising from the bed every morning?"

She stood and walked around the table. "I beg your pardon, my lord, but I must return to my maid. I promised Mr. Hitchcock's daughter I would be gone only a short while. Come, Ursa." She dipped a small curtsy and left the room, throwing a wave to her grooms, who had stood the moment she did.

Casting one more look in Dash's direction, the dog followed. Its eyes were definitely hostile.

The men settled back in their chairs.

Dash turned to them. "Miss Talcott must be a good employer."

"The best."

"None better."

"As I thought. Tell me about that dog. It looks like a bear."

The taller of the grooms scratched his shoulder. "That be Ursa, some Newfriend or somethin'. Big, but friendly."

The other groom shook his head. "Newfoundland. Don't wanna tangle with 'im, though. No, indeed."

Ursa, indeed. Exquisitely apropos. Dash returned to his plate and worked through almost all of it, washing down the last bite with the remainder of his ale.

He had no desire for any wilderness adventure. Not in the slightest. If he wanted to do something useful, he ought to teach Miss Talcott to loosen her stays and learn to enjoy herself. Her looks were rather plain, but she had large, luminous, arresting eyes. With a maid, two grooms, and what he remembered as a sturdy equippage and team out in the yard, she obviously had means. And she needed a little excitement in her life, excitement he could show her, as long as Ursa kept his distance.

Hitchcock set another foaming tankard before him and Dash took a deep swallow. London was a wilderness, was it not? Not the kind of wilderness he originally had in mind, but if his cronies gave him a hard time, he could develop an ideal definition. So perhaps he would conduct his wilderness adventure in the wilds of the great city.

Anne felt Lord Daniel's eyes follow her out of the room. She really should not have spoken with him, but how could she ignore his presence when he introduced himself? She had already known who he was, the second son of the Duke of Granum. His arrival at the inn had sent Mr. Hitchcock and his family into paroxysms of excitement. Her grooms had greatly praised his horse as the finest prime blood. She had not noticed. With that disgraceful man on his back, the animal had looked equally disreputable.

However, Lord Daniel's appearance in the taproom

was altogether different. With the benefit of a few hours' rest, he looked quite, ah, handsome, did he not? And his apologies seemed sincere. He was all that was polite.

But he was the very worst kind of wastrel, precisely the kind she vowed to ignore in London.

Ursa followed her into Mary's room. Anne motioned Emmy to go, whispering her thanks while the maid seemed deep in slumber. Anne touched the back of her hand to Mary's forehead, pleased to find it much cooler.

Anne sat in the chair where she had already spent so many hours. Ursa propped his muzzle on her knee and closed his eyes in rapture as she scratched his ears. She let her thoughts turn back to the man downstairs. Yes, very good looking, but probably spoiled and profligate, growing up where he had too much of everything, too much money and too many people waiting on him. And she doubted he ever had any responsibilities, either.

Lord Daniel was exactly the opposite of the kind of man she sought as a husband. She had high hopes of meeting her Ideal in London. In character he would be much like Mr. Lambert, the vicar at home, who made his hopes of wedding her more than obvious. Mr. Lambert was a moral, upstanding man, sober and learned. She certainly admired him, but found no spark there, no possibility of the love she wished she might feel. Even his kindness to children did not earn him a spot in her heart.

The man she sought might combine the physical characteristics of Lord Daniel with the intellect of Mr. Lambert. Lord Daniel's fine eyes and sheepish smile, his wide shoulders and long legs . . . the vision brought a warm flush to Anne's face. She certainly hoped he would be on his way before she came down tomorrow.

* * *

Dash woke to the sounds of activity in the coachyard, the shouts of an ostler, the jangle of harness, the snorting and stamping of horses. He rolled over and turned his face into the pillow against the light. The ache in his head was tamer, but he felt groggy and sluggish. It had taken a half dozen tankards of ale to get those grooms to reveal Miss Talcott's London direction. He pulled the covers over his head to block out the noise and tried to fall back into sleep.

Give her about two weeks in London, two weeks of dreary lectures and dull salons, lackluster balls and tedious squeezes. She would welcome his attention and a little excitement in her life. Dash remembered Easterly and his silly young wife, a henwit if there ever was one. As companion to Sarah, Miss Talcott would be more than ready for some real entertainment.

Meanwhile, he would rusticate for a while. Let Julie, Fan, and Harry double the size of their bets. His old pals would argue endlessly about the wager, or he missed his guess.

Even through the blankets he could hear the high-pitched voices of women in the yard below. Very slowly, careful not to jar his head, he went to the window and peered out. Indeed, Miss Talcott's party, including a figure swathed in blankets, was on the point of leaving.

Dash gave a little laugh. After she had enough time to learn how very tiresome Society could be, he would find her and show her what fun was all about. An interesting challenge, one that ought to occupy him for a few amusing weeks.

Chapter Two

Dash glanced over the inhabitants of the coffee room and picked out Sir Pembroke Fletcher as his target. The lanky baronet sat alone with the newspaper and a glass of claret.

Dash ambled over and sat down beside him. "G'evening, Fletcher."

"Felicitations, Dash. Thought you was hiding in the hills."

"Amazin' how the silliest rumors catch hold." Dash knew only the slightest push was necessary to get Flectcher talking. "What do you say of the Season so far? Did I not hear that Easterly's widow is back on the town?"

Sir Pembroke's thin, nasal voice rose in glee. "Ah, indeed, the delectable widow's return! She is rich, lovely, and quite dim-witted, more eagerly courted than any lady in town. Don't tell me you have an interest there?"

"Hardly. Has she a companion?"

"Indeed, a cousin, I believe. They are bound to be at the Lelands' this evening as will you and I, *n'est-ce pas*?

Dash shrugged. "Perhaps."

"And that reminds me. Heard you gave your bit o' muslin her congé, ain't that so?"

"That is ancient history, Flectcher. Stale as last week's ale."

Several hours later, clad in flawless evening attire, Dash walked into the Lelands' crowded ballroom, well after the names were no longer being announced. He let himself become accustomed to the noise level for a moment, then sauntered toward Gregory, Lord Fancourt, one of Dash's closest circle.

Fancourt lifted one eyebrow in surprise. "Thought you was hiding in a cottage somewhere, Dash."

"Not at all. I said I needed a wilderness. After two tame weeks in Derbyshire, London fits the bill as the wildest place I know."

Fancourt cuffed him on the shoulder. He turned to follow Dash's example and scanned the crowd. "Who is that young lady in the green standing beside Lady Orcutt?"

Dash located the slender figure of the miss in question. "I have no idea. I don't recall seeing her, unless . . ."

"Unless what?"

Unless she is Miss Talcott. Dash did not answer, simply walked away from Fancourt and toward the lady in pale green. Indeed, as he moved closer, he saw Miss Talcott had changed herself from a plain-faced harridan to an angel rivaling anyone in the room for beauty, style and grace, an astonishing transformation.

Before she noticed him, Dash slid behind a group of elderly gentlemen. He needed a few moments to reorder his plans. He had pictured Miss Talcott in a sober, high-necked gown, her hair in that tight bun, quite out of place in a tonnish ballroom. Instead she stood out as would a pearl in a basket of beach pebbles.

He took up a position where he could watch her from behind a screen of people. As soon as they announced the next set, two gentlemen appeared at her side. He watched her shake her head and smile as if saying she could not possibly choose between them. Lord Ingram, another of Dash's best friends, suddenly stood between the two losers and bowed low. Miss Talcott curtsied, placed her hand on Ingram's arm, and followed him to the floor. A stab of envy made Dash lift a glass of champagne from a passing footman's tray.

Drat the luck. If Ingram chose her as a partner, she was already a success, for his friend, the viscount, never wasted his allure on inferior females.

He watched and waited as the set continued into another song and new pattern of steps. Within a few moments, he saw her step aside and speak to Ingram, who led her out of the formation and toward the champagne fountain.

Dash set his empty glass on a table and strolled forward, intercepting them near the refreshments. "Good evening."

Miss Talcott looked at him with dawning recognition in her eyes.

Ingram immediately did the honors. "Miss Talcott, may I make known to you my very good friend Lord Daniel Dashworth? Dash, I have the honor of introducing Miss Anne Talcott."

Dash bowed low to her curtsy. "I am your servant, Miss Talcott."

Her cheeks appeared to be tinged with a darker shade of rose than a moment ago, Dash thought. But her big gray eyes, sparkling in the light of the chandelier overhead, had the same cool, appraising character he remembered from the little inn.

"Are you enjoying London, Miss Talcott?"

"I have enjoyed the last few weeks."

They were joined by several of Dash's friends, who

gradually moved between Dash and Miss Talcott. It took him several moments to work around to her side again.

He gave her his most generous smile. "I see you have taken my advice and decided to enjoy London to the utmost."

"I cannot imagine what you mean. Your advice was of the most appalling sort, Lord Daniel. I would never consider remembering anything you said."

He kept his laughter low and intimate. "But you are lovely; you are transformed."

"I cannot think what you mean. If I look different tonight than I looked while tramping through the forest clothed in a traveling outfit meant to provide practical comfort, it should come as no surprise." Her words were at odds with the smile on her lips, her very moist and tempting lips.

"How very true." He laughed again. He liked the way she brought him to laughter. Camilla, his never-missed former mistress, had never made him laugh, though she had more than adequately serviced other of his needs. "So your program of improving activities has made you happy?"

"I am trying to help my cousin, who is eager to throw off her sadness after her husband's death last year. She chooses to have a bit of gaiety before we undertake more edifying endeavors."

Dash smiled and felt sure he could see her react to the power of his charm by tilting her head and widening her smile. "Perhaps you would accompany me for a turn around the park someday?"

"I should like that very much, Lord Daniel."

He leaned closer and whispered. "You did not tell Lord Ingram we had already met."

"Nor did you." Her eyes twinkled with merriment.

Again, the circle around them shifted and they were moved far apart. But Dash considered his goal achieved. Tomorrow he would call on her and set a date for their ride.

The moment the carriage door closed and they moved off, Sarah threw her arms around Anne and squealed in delight. "Anne, you have made another conquest!"

"Do not be ridiculous, Cousin Sarah! If a man so much as gives me a nod, you declare him besmitten."

"Lord Daniel looked like a man who yearned for your smile! I saw you two whispering and laughing while everyone else was talking."

Anne shook her head and moved away from her cousin, pulling a lap robe over her knees. "You were busy with Lord Rossiter. I cannot imagine you saw anything of the kind."

Sarah waved her hands in dismissal. "If you are so foolish as to ignore every hint a man gives you, he might not come around again. Just wait until you see who sends posies tomorrow."

Anne did not choose to tell Sarah about her commitment to ride in the park with Lord Daniel. Not yet, anyway. Sarah's extravagant imagination would turn it into a near betrothal.

For once Sarah seemed more interested in Anne's evening than her own. "You know they call him Dash."

"The temptation would be irresistible, no doubt."

"You know why he is known as Dash, then?"

Anne rolled her eyes. "Because it is his name?"

Sarah gave a trill of laughter. "Because he cuts a dash. He is a scamp, one of those handsome rogues women cannot refuse. And I think he has set his eye on you, Anne. I declare I am envious. He is much better looking than Lord Rossiter."

"Ah, but not so rich, I am sure."

"Darling Richard is certainly plump in the pocket, as the saying goes. But Dash is perfect for a little fling. He will never marry, at least not for many years. I suspect he is having too much fun."

Sarah's words remained in Anne's thoughts as she prepared for bed in the house she resided in with her father, Baron Talcott. *Dash will never marry . . . have a little fling . . . too much fun . . .*

Anne sat at her dressing table and braided her remaining long hair. The front had been cut short and left to curl around her face. The tresses in the back were easiest to keep untangled if she braided them at night. Though she had been distraught when Monsieur insisted on cutting it, the curls turned her mousy light brown hair to a flattering honey gold near her cheeks.

London had turned out to be very different than what she had expected. Her father intended her to spend almost every evening with her cousin, and Sarah was determined to dance until the wee hours. There had been no time for the sightseeing Anne yearned for. And though she had a few ladies coming tomorrow for a literary discussion, she had not attended a single talk by an eminent personage.

Nor had there been any men she considered suitable as a prospective match. The men were often sillier than the ladies, fixating on neckties or the gloss of their boots. None of Sarah's acquaintances talked about anything more substantive than fashion and gossip. Anne hoped that once Sarah had her fill of gaiety, they might find a few events of more cerebral substance.

"Ursa." The dog came immediately to her and stared at her with his big sad eyes. She rubbed his neck and scratched his ears. "Poor darling. This is no place for an outdoor fellow like you, is it? A few walks in the park do not compare with running free, my pet." Despite his usually correct behavior, Ursa was no favorite of the household staff, neither the footmen who were sent out to walk him several times a day nor the maids who picked his dark hairs from the furniture and rugs.

Anne rubbed her cheek against Ursa's head. "I miss the country too, sweetling. A sedate carriage ride will never make up for a good gallop through the fields for either of us."

She hated to seem ungrateful to Sarah, for without her, Anne would have stayed home most evenings while her father attended political dinners or sessions in the House. That Sarah preferred only the most frivolous of entertainments did not mean London was a complete disappointment. Acquiring a new wardrobe and visiting the many shops and warehouses had been enjoyable for a few days. Perhaps the absence of suitable gentlemen bothered Anne most. Those she met seemed frivolous fellows, much like Lord Daniel.

It was kind of him to invite her to ride in the park. Usually she went along with Sarah and her cadre of admirers. But this might be different, being away from Sarah's orbit. Of course, Dash's good looks had absolutely nothing to do with her eagerness.

Nor did the little thrill of anticipation she felt each time she thought of him have any real danger for her. She was quite positive she knew the difference between a man worth marrying and one who was nothing but a rascal.

Dash felt rather proud of his ingenuity in making instant alterations to his plans for Miss Talcott. He had

changed his plan right on the spot. He had planned to
introduce Miss Talcott to the excitement of London, anticipated changing a quiet, unattractive young woman
into a Toast by taking her to the most capable modistes.
He intended to pay attention to her and thus lend her his
consequence, which would bring her the attention of
many gentlemen. Any female Dash favored with his notice would be well on her way to the esteem of the *beau
monde*. He looked forward to the challenge. But instead
of the dour spinster he expected, Anne Talcott was already admired for her beauty and sought after by men
such as his friends Ingram and Fancourt.

So he revised his strategy to a more pleasant aim, to
make her London stay memorable and help her find a
good match, if finding a husband was her true desire.

Never let it be said, he thought to himself, that Dashworth was a slowtop when it came to finding the way to
a lady's service.

"Is Miss Talcott at home?"

Baron Talcott's starchy butler could not hide his cha-
grin when he accepted Dash's calling card and ostensibly
went off to see if Miss Talcott was in. What the man really was doing, Dash knew, was checking to see if Miss
Talcott wanted to see this unexpected arrival.

A long, mournful howl erupted from the depths of
the house. Dash whirled around, then immediately realized it must be that big, gruff dog, apparently banished
to the basement.

The butler looked even more disgruntled when he
came downstairs, handed Dash's walking stick, hat,
and gloves to a footman, and led Dash up to the drawing room.

"Lord Daniel Dashworth."

At the butler's words, the high-pitched buzz of ladies' voices stopped all at once and Dash was greeted with total silence and a roomful of inquisitive faces.

Miss Talcott arose and came to him. "Good day, Lord Daniel. It is a pleasure to see you." Her voice was polite, if cool.

"Have I interrupted something? If so, I can return at a more convenient time."

"Not at all. We are discussing the latest novel by Mrs. Edgeworth, but we have almost completed our observations. Please let me introduce you to my friends."

Dash survived a flurry of introductions to six ladies of varying ages, sizes, and shapes. The conversation resumed in myriad sections, as if all the ladies spoke at once. In a dizzying half hour, they thrust Dash from one conversation to another without his knowing to which subject he was supposed to contribute.

When only Mrs. Ambrose and Lady Winifred remained in the corner, he could at last sit beside Miss Talcott. She was very fetching in a pale blue gown, and he again reminded himself of the awful moment when he had seen her wrapped in a dark cloak and thought her one of the village crones.

"You are looking quite the picture of tonnish elegance this afternoon. No one would suspect you are a budding bluestocking."

"Why, thank you for the compliments, Lord Daniel. I fear I have neither the intellect nor the acumen to deserve such a designation. I believe the ladies known as bluestockings take great pride in their abilities and their conduct, which is of the highest moral distinction. Is that not your impression?"

"Miss Talcott, you shame me. I fear my acquaintance

with such ladies is entirely based on rumor and the gossip of worthless nodcocks like myself. If I knew a bluestocking, I would most eagerly introduce you. Sadly, my crowd tends to be rather weak in the intellect department."

Anne directly met his eyes. "Perhaps you slander your friends as well as yourself, Lord Daniel. Or are you fishing for a flattering dissent from me?"

"I find your frankness a most refreshing characteristic, so I hardly expect any disagreement about the scarcity of my wits."

"Then I shall give you none." She raised her eyebrows as if expecting a rebuttal.

Instead Dash gave her another of his most celebrated grins. "I beg your pardon for spoiling your literary discussion."

"Not at all. Most had expressed their opinions and had begun to dwell on specific interpretations which could well have caused a spat if you had not arrived when you did."

"That relieves my conscience."

She laughed softly.

"Apparently your dog is unhappy about his exclusion from the conversation."

"Poor Ursa. Mrs. Rice is beside herself. He has already dug up part of the garden, and helped himself to an entire fowl from her larder, as well as one of the cakes she baked for this afternoon."

Dash shook his head. "He is rather large for a house pet, is he not?"

"Yes. He needs space to run. A walk around the square only whets his appetite."

The vision of his friend's villa near the village of Hampstead tickled Dash's consciousness. "Could you tolerate having him put out to pasture, so to speak, just for a few weeks? I have a place in mind where he could run about, and we could visit him frequently."

"Oh, Lord Daniel, what a wonderful idea!"

"Why, Miss Talcott, I do believe I have inspired you to give me a most flirtatious smile."

Her eyes widened in disbelief. "I never flirt!"

He leaned closer. "Perfect. Open your eyes a bit wider and peer up at me. Quite perfect."

"Oh, do not be so silly."

"Yes, Miss Talcott. You could offer lessons to other young ladies."

"Please stop, I implore you."

"The ideal request. Here I thought you were in need of instruction in flirting, and you are the model of technique."

She clapped her mouth shut and frowned at him. "If I were not a lady entertaining guests . . ."

"In fact, the epitome of skill. Are the men of your neighborhood equally adept at courting?"

"Not that I have noticed." She managed to adopt a prim demeanor and a stern cast to her expression.

Dash grinned. "Then what a waste of your talents. Now, would this arrangement for the dog please you?"

Her face returned to a pleasant smile. "Yes. I would be delighted to improve Ursa's accommodations."

"Then I shall call for both of you at four."

Dash whistled a bit as he went down the stairs, accepted his things from the butler, and dropped a coin into the fellow's hand. There were many ways to earn a butler's favor. Or a lady's.

Chapter Three

Dash looked up from his newspaper at the sound of familiar voices in the hall of his club. For the last hour he had anticipated the arrival of his three best friends. He was ready for them.

He folded the paper and, with studied nonchalance, strolled into the dining room and pulled out the fourth chair at their table as though he was expected to occupy it.

"Dash!" Lord Julian Rowland was the most surprised of the three to see him. "What in thunder are you doin' here? Thought you was playin' hermit out in the highlands."

Harry Ingram rubbed his hands together as if contemplating a table covered with gold coins instead of white linen. "Naw. That's the whole point of this meeting, Julie, to settle our bets. Ol' Dash didn't last a fortnight in the woods. You owe me forty guineas."

Dash listened in silence.

Lord Julian's face wrinkled into a scowl. "That much? Was I foxed?"

"Yes, we was all foxed. Dash worst of all."

Greg Fancourt grinned and wiggled his eyebrows. "Silence, you two popinjays. Maybe there ain't no settlement to be had."

"What do you mean?" Harry bristled. "Dash said he'd be gone for months and here he is already, two weeks later, sitting in St. James Street, large as life."

"Ah, but do you recall what we laid our wagers on? That he would stay in the wilderness till June, I believe." Fan's smirk amused Dash so that he could hardly keep a straight face.

Julie's phiz looked even more comical.

"Wilderness. Don't that mean rough country, hills and mountains and such?"

Fan gestured to Dash. "Explain yourself to them, man."

"As I said to Fan last night, I did not define wilderness. I spent two weeks amongst the crags of Derbyshire but found it extremely dull. For out and out wildness, what can top London?"

His statement brought identical moans of dismay from both Julie and Harry.

"That ain't fair," Harry muttered.

Fan held up one hand to silence the others. "I have an alternative proposal, an extension of our wager."

Ingram and Julie all snapped to attention, speaking in unison. "Yes?"

Dash started to speak, then decided to hold his tongue.

When Fan had their full attention, he cleared his throat and spoke with exaggerated self-importance. "I will take your wagers opposing my bet that Dash will end up losing his heart this Season."

"What?" The word exploded from Dash. "Are you dicked in the nob? My heart?"

"Who is the lucky miss?" Julie's face showed his surprise. "He ain't been partial to anyone for years, as I recall."

Dash slapped his hand on the table. "The lady I spoke

to last night, Fan, is Miss Talcott, who has not been in town before. I was merely being polite."

Lord Julian stared at Dash for a moment. "I won't throw good money after bad, but if you let the previous sum ride, I cannot do worse than I already have."

Dash shook his head in mock despair. "You fellows are as ramshackle a trio as ever it has been my misfortune to know. I am so convinced you are a bunch of windbags without a clue to my interests that I will take on all your bets."

"What? We'll all bet you fall for her?"

"You that sure you can avoid that pretty miss?"

Dash gave a disdainful snort. "I am so certain of my safety that I will even double your sums if you win." He sat back with satisfaction, watching the surprised faces of his friends. They would be sadly distraught when he proved himself correct and filled his purse with their guineas.

"It was very kind of you to burden your friend with Ursa, Lord Daniel."

With Anne sitting beside him in his curricle, Dash drove his favorite pair toward Mayfair in the late afternoon sunshine. His friend Freddy Eckford had been more than willing to give Ursa the run of his property. "My pleasure, Miss Talcott. But don't worry about a burden to him. As you saw, Freddy stables some of my horses and keeps them fit. He will do the same for Ursa."

"I insist upon providing him with compensation, Lord Daniel." She placed her hand on his forearm as if to reinforce the sincerity of her words.

"As I told you before, that subject is forbidden."

"But I—"

"I pay Freddy for his services, which now include caring for Ursa. You need not concern yourself with matters such as fees."

"Then I thank you even more, though it is quite unnecessary for you to pay for Ursa's care." She withdrew her hand and slid a little farther away from him.

"You are most welcome." He wondered if he took the reins in one hand and put his arm around her if she would move back until they were thigh to thigh. No, not Miss Talcott. She was much too proper.

"Why do you keep so many horses in town?"

He knew she would not approve of his frequent competitive sprints, battles on the Brighton road, or races with the Royal Mail coach. "I make them available to my brother." It was a lie, but a small one.

"How do you amuse yourself?"

He glanced over at her and gave her a wink and a smile. "I spend a great deal of time, ah, well, playing cards."

"And I suppose you practice boxing. Never say you go to mills."

"Well, I have been known to attend a mill in my day. But for myself, I prefer fencing."

He loved the look of surprise on her face. She was quite extraordinarily pretty. "Fencing? That sounds very old-fashioned."

Her straw bonnet framed her face and acted to emphasize her eyes, a most charming picture. "I find practice matches keep my eye sharp and my reactions quick."

"Your life must be quite dull."

"What? My life dull?" The very idea seemed ridiculous.

"Are you interested in the stars? Or in electricity? Or in discoveries? Or in traveling?"

He focused his attention the road and the pair for a moment, then stole another look at her. "I travel to my hunting box a few times a year. I will probably go to Brighton later in the summer." He had never considered himself susceptible to females who had her sweet innocent vulnerability, but somehow Miss Talcott seemed both delectable and desirable.

"Have you been to Paris?"

Was that a note of longing in her voice? "Last year I started out to cross the channel, but we were twice delayed, first by fog, then by heavy storms. Gave up and came back to town."

Her eyes filled with amazement. "You were on your way to Paris and let a little delay stop you? Gracious, Lord Daniel."

He realized he had perhaps gone too far. "I shall visit Paris soon. Such an important journey should have a propitious beginning, do you not agree?"

"Yes, but if I were to have such an opportunity, that in itself would be favorable enough!"

"Yes, so I should have thought." He remembered, however, a decidedly unfavorable aching head after two days spent in a Dover inn imbibing a variety of spirits out of little but boredom. Retreating to London had been wiser than adding seasickness to his difficulties.

The conversation was not going well. He needed a new topic of discourse.

"Do you ride, Miss Talcott?"

"Yes, of course. Why do you ask?"

"I though you might enjoy going to visit Ursa tomorrow on horseback. We can take him for a run on the Heath."

"That sounds very nice, Lord Daniel."

Dash gave himself a mental pat on the back as he guided the horses past a little church tucked back into the trees. Miss Talcott heaved such a loud sigh he was taken aback. "You sound distressed. Is something wrong?"

"Oh, no, not exactly. Just looking at that church reminds me of, ah, reminds me of home."

"And you yearn for your familiar places?"

"Not at all. It was merely a bit of . . ." Her voice quieted into silence.

"A bit of?" he echoed.

"Nothing. I was letting my mind wander."

"And it was an unfortunate thought that wandered into your head? You sounded quite forlorn."

"I beg your pardon. It is nothing you need be concerned with."

He pulled the horses to a stop and turned to her.

"Miss Talcott, I do not allow my passengers to be unhappy. Either you shall rid yourself of your melancholy or I shall have to set you down to walk back."

She tried to laugh, but it was a feeble attempt. "You seem determined, my lord, to interfere in my most private thoughts."

"Interfere? Certainly not! I need only remind you that confession is said to be good for the soul." He found himself truly curious about what she was thinking.

"Oh, you are a wretched pest! You will laugh if I tell you why my spirits plummeted when we passed that little church."

"I promise I shall be all that is serious."

"You see, the church made me think of Mr. Lambert, vicar of our parish."

"A thought unpleasant enough to cast you into the sullens?"

"No. Rather, yes. You see, I find Mr. Lambert to be a pattern card of respectability, a man of morality and an upstanding gentleman. But I do not care for him—that is, in a romantic way."

Dash nodded, seeing clearly where she was headed. "He has developed a *tendre* for you, I see. But you do not wish to become Mrs. Lambert?"

She nodded. "You are correct. It is most provoking. Mr. Lambert is all I require in a husband. It is just that he is not . . . oh, I should not be sharing my thoughts with you, my lord. How very unseemly of me!"

"Not at all. I flatter myself to think we have become friends, Miss Talcott, even after meeting under the most inauspicious of circumstances. I find it entirely fitting that you tell me of your concerns." He could never remember a similar thought, not even when the conversation about potential husbands was carried on by his own sisters.

She did not speak for a few moments.

He took her hand. "I take it that you cannot confide in Lady Easterly?"

"Sarah believes all problems can be solved by engaging in a waltz with a willing partner."

"For Sarah, I expect that is true, Miss Talcott. But surely you have met many eligible men in London?"

She let him hold one hand while she played with the fringe on her parasol with the other. "Eligible, perhaps, in some ways."

"How do you measure a man? By what standards do you assess his suitability?" Again, he was struck by how unusual his interest was. What did it matter what kind of man appealed to Miss Talcott?

"Oh, there are only a very few, as far as I am concerned. I admire men of moral conviction, with serious purpose for their lives. I think of how he would be as a father to the children I hope to have someday . . ." Again her voice faded.

"And you have not found such men in London?"

"Oh, I have no idea. That is the problem. How might one ascertain the deeper nature of a gentleman while engaged in the trivialities of the Season's amusements?"

Dash shook his head, as if reproving her. "Why, those trivialities provide the spice of life! You are a spirited young lady who needs no lessons in behavior from the likes of me. I can tell you enjoy laughter and fun. You need to seek those qualities in your future husband as well as a proclivity toward more serious pursuits."

Dash watched her smile slowly surface.

"There you are, Miss Talcott. The advice of a fribble brings you a grin. You cannot ever again pretend to be a bookish, prudish sourpuss. I know better."

She sputtered a little, then laughed outright. "You are saying I am not what I wish to be. Not only am I mistaken in my quest for a man of propriety, I do not even know my own mind."

"All I know is that you are now smiling, yet a few moments ago when you were thinking about sober and morally upright men, you were frowning. Now hold on to that smile, if you please." Dash called to his pair, "Walk on."

Anne perched on a chair in Lady Grenfell's drawing room and tried to concentrate on the discussion. A lady was extolling the virtues of some poet named Wainwright. The speaker felt the poet's lack of reputation was an indictment of the taste of the entire British nation.

But Anne's mind kept taking her back to the afternoon in Dash's curricle and the advice he offered her regarding prospective husbands. She had chosen to be here at the literary gathering tonight instead of at the Templemans' rout with Sarah. Dash would have been at the Templemans' too.

"Mr. Wainwright's point," the speaker droned, "is that life takes unexpected turns, and he goes on to imply . . ."

Yes, Anne thought, unexpected turns indeed. Dash's kindness to Ursa was commendable. And truly unexpected. Equally unexpected had been his advice on the qualities she should look for in the choice of a husband, advice by his own admission from a fribble.

Yet did he deserve his own opinion of himself? Dash's good looks, charm, and distinguished family probably got him everything in life he desired. Was that a good foundation for disapproving of him? Anne liked to think she was tolerant and accepting, considerate of everyone. Certainly her toleration could extend to a rich and well-born young man who had been overindulged since birth.

She wondered which young ladies he might entertain this evening. Perhaps he would play cards. Anne had not revealed to anyone, not her father, not even Sarah, that she had long ago learned several card games. Her mother, rest her poor soul, would have been scandalized. So far in London, she had not been tempted into a game. But at a table with Dash . . . whatever was she thinking? Her childish skills, so long neglected, would be laughable.

"Wainwright's last lines take us deep into the investigation of self-knowledge . . ."

Self-knowledge, indeed, Anne thought with a pang. Here she was, supposedly fulfilling her most earnest desire for intellectual exchange, but in truth wishing she could be playing a card game with a young man who did not take himself seriously. Perhaps his self-knowledge was faulty, but she obviously did not know herself at all.

The next morning, Dash yawned a little as he mounted Ajax. Perhaps he had been foolish to stay at the Templemans' so late last night. He took a lead rein for the little gray mare from the groom and urged Ajax into the street. He had certainly known Miss Talcott would not come to the ball if she was not there by eleven.

He refused to allow himself to refine upon yesterday's conversations with Miss Talcott. His interest in her was quite unprecedented, some sort of passing fancy he would soon discard. He assured himself of the ephemeral nature of his interest as he approached her house.

But when he saw her come down the steps dressed in a handsome riding habit, he had to admit she was a fine sight. He complimented her on the little shako with its curving feathers. "You look bright and sporting this morning, Miss Talcott, and I particularly favor that hat!"

She blushed a little and murmured her thanks. "This outfit is one of the extravagances Sarah required me to order. I had doubted I would have an opportunity to wear it, but now I shall have to express my appreciation for her insistence."

Dash led the gray to her. "This little mare is Dusty, and I guarantee her good manners." He cupped his hands and, when Anne placed her foot in them, raised her up to the saddle.

"Very good, Lord Daniel. Again, I thank you."

For a few moments as they negotiated the busy

streets, Dash watched closely to see that Anne knew what she was about on horseback. As usual with the lady, Dash was more than satisfied at her equestrian prowess.

When the traffic thinned out on the route to Hampstead, he complimented her on her riding skill. "You have a good seat and fine hands, Miss Talcott."

She turned toward him with a look of surprise. "Did I not tell you I rode, Lord Daniel?"

"Yes, but there are riders and then there are horsewomen. I would place you among the latter. And I wish you would call me Dash. Lord Daniel is what my father calls me when he takes me to task for various lapses in my conduct."

When they arrived at Freddy's yard, Ursa nearly turned himself inside out in his joy to see his mistress, pawing at her long velvet skirt and snuffling at her face. Anne was a picture of joy herself, smiling and hugging the beast.

For Dash, the dog had a menacing look, a curl of his lip, and a rumbling series of growls. *Just desserts for my efforts to keep you out of trouble,* Dash said to the dog, if silently. But as long as Anne was happy—and the dog kept his distance—Dash had no second thoughts.

Ursa adored his mistress with worshipful devotion, following her every move with eyes full of love. Dash wished he knew how to give his own eyes that passionate, soulful look. No female could have resisted.

Once the greetings were completed, they cantered off through fields and toward Hampstead Heath. Ursa ran ahead of them most of the time, occasionally turning away to follow some scent until Miss Talcott whistled him back.

When they reached the top of the hill, they slowed the

horses to a walk. Dash waved toward a grove of trees. "There is a wonderful view of the city over there beyond the woods. Would you like to see it?"

"Yes. I believe I am a country girl at heart, but there are many things I enjoy in the city."

Dash laughed. "And from a distance, with all the imperfections blurred, it is particularly beautiful."

Just before the full view unfolded, they stopped and dismounted, winding the reins around the branch of a tree. Ursa had taken one of his excursions in pursuit of a hare, so they were alone as Dash offered his arm and they walked a few steps into the grass.

Dash watched her face as he spoke. "Behold, the metropolis of London."

Rays of sunshine showered the distant dome of St. Paul's and gleamed on distant roofs. Anne shook her head in wonder, eyes shining, cheeks rosy, and lips trembling. "It is breathtaking, like a miniature city made of spun sugar. I never imagined there would be such a place as this."

Dash tucked her arm tighter against his side. "Once the haunt of highwaymen, feared by every coachman coming into town." He dropped his voice to a whispery, menacing basso. "The outlaws hid in the brush and when the coach approached, they sprang out and grabbed the horses' heads. 'Stand and deliver,' they shouted."

Anne shuddered and he pulled her even closer, wrapping his arm around her.

"When the passengers climbed out, they gave up everything, even their rings and brooches, their purses, baggage, and the mail. Oh, them were wicked days!"

She turned her face to his and grinned. "But they never imposed on the ladies?"

"Not their stock in trade. Though I've heard tell of

some ladies who fancied a kiss from the Ghostly Gentleman James."

"Shocking!"

Their lips were only inches apart. He ran a fingertip down the side of her cheek, then tipped up her chin. Very slowly he lowered his lips to hers, feeling their soft warmth and wishing the moment might never end.

"Only a kiss, never a lady's virtue." Dash moved back slightly. "Our Gentleman James faded away into the darkness, and it is said he never took a wedding ring."

"Whatever happened to him?" Her voice was whispery, breathless.

"The stories have no ending. Perhaps he was hanged at Tyburn. Perhaps he went to the colonies." He gave another low laugh. "More likely he had full entrée to London drawing rooms and married a rich widow."

She gasped, then giggled, still nestled against him.

He brushed his lips across her forehead. "Now I must confess to entirely improper behavior and whisk you back to Mayfair."

She laughed coyly. "You mean a kiss is the crowning moment for every lady you bring here?"

He clasped her hand in his and raised it to his lips. "Only this kind of kiss, perhaps, Miss Talcott."

Suddenly, Anne shoved him aside. He caught just a flash of black racing toward them.

Anne placed herself in front of him and called out. "Here, Ursa, come to me."

The dog slowed his headlong pace and swerved past her, almost rolling over in his attempt to stop. She knelt on the grass and wrapped her arms around his neck.

Dash drew a breath and spoke in what he hoped would be a normal voice. "Do I deduce the noble Ursa was bounding over here in order to make mincemeat of my limbs?"

She looked up at him with a frightened half smile. Her bonnet had been knocked off and her disheveled hair flew in the breeze. "I fear you are correct, Lord Daniel. I truly apologize."

"No need whatsoever, Miss Talcott. The tragedy was averted due to your quick reaction. I fear Ursa simply misconstrued the nature of my—or should I say *our*?— activities."

Keeping a close watch on the panting beast, Dash untied the horses and helped Anne to remount. The dog growled a little, but was silenced by just a word from her.

"Ursa!" Her voice was strong and firm.

Clearly, Dash thought, the next time he chose to kiss the lady, it would be well away from the damned dog.

Anne watched in the looking glass as Mary arranged her honey ringlets. She was certain she must look different now that she had been introduced to the exhilarating sensations caused by a man's kiss. Her lips still tingled from Dash's touch a few hours ago. Or at least it felt so to Anne's imagination.

Her maid knew nothing of the fascinating man Anne had met while poor Mary lay ill at that little inn. Anne assumed Mary reported everything she learned about her mistress's dreams and desires to Mrs. Rice, the housekeeper, who in turn would tell her father. So Anne dared not ask Mary if she had changed in appearance since that morning. What would her father say if he knew Anne had been far off on Hampstead Heath this afternoon with a man whose rakish reputation was well known?

For the most part, Baron Talcott was as tolerant and forbearing a father as her late mother had been exacting and scrupulously correct. Since Anne arrived in London, she saw him in the house from time to time, but he spent most of his time either at his club or at the House. He expected her to spend her evenings with Sarah, whose widowed state qualified her as something of a chaperon. He had no idea that Sarah looked upon Anne as simply a partner in finding the gayest, most sparkling entertainments almost every evening. Once rid of her dull husband, Sarah had become quite the socialite.

As Mary twisted a final curl beside her face, Anne yearned to be alone, to have the silence and serenity with which to confront her muddled and complicated thoughts. Finally, the maid pronounced herself satisfied with Anne's appearance and left the room, though not before warning her mistress she had only a half hour before the carriage would arrive to take her and Sarah to the Cuthberts' ball.

Anne drew a deep breath and stared into the mirror, bringing the candles closer so she could examine her lips, her cheeks, her eyes. She felt different, but the alteration did not seem evident on her face.

How could this be? For many years, she had dreamed of being kissed. Now she expected to see the news written all over her face. Instead, there were the same gray eyes, the same smooth cheeks, the same mouth. She licked her lips, thinking they felt no different either.

But inside she had changed forever. All she had to do was think of Dash's face coming close to hers and her knees went weak, her nerves tingled, and her insides felt all warm and mushy.

Oh, she should have pushed him away, perhaps slapped him, shown him her resistance.

Except her resistance never materialized. She had leaned on his arm and offered herself willingly. How could she have been so foolish, so imprudent, so very easy?

If it had not been for Ursa's near attack, she might be still be in Dash's arms, out there on the hill overlooking the city.

Perhaps she was lucky the dog had interrupted them. Otherwise, who knew what could have happened? But once Ursa made his attitude so obvious, Dash would have been a fool to kiss her again.

He had regained his composure much faster than she had. As they rode back to town, he had told her more stories about highwaymen, not a word of which she could now recall. By the time they reached Mayfair, she had been composed, though still embarrassed.

She stared into the mirror and rearranged her pearl necklace. Unless her eyes deceived her, no one tonight would learn her new and secret status from her looks.

Dash was a charming rascal, no doubt about it. His advice to her yesterday about finding a husband who was more than sober and morally upright, one who had a sense of humor, made good sense.

She needed to add to her list of requirements. But how did one find such a man? Someplace between the sobriety of Mr. Lambert and the feckless humor and irresponsibility of Dash.

Yet Dash was not irresponsible, was he? He had been concerned for Ursa's comfort, even though he had kept an apprehensive eye on the dog all the way out to Freddy Eckford's place yesterday. No, he had been all kindness. And look how he was repaid by her silly dog. Ursa had been within a hair of knocking him flat.

Anne rose from her dressing table and walked over to

the cheval glass and looked at her reflection, from the flower-decked topknot on her head to the toes of her silver slippers. The dress had a modest neckline compared to most of Sarah's, but Anne tugged it upward anyway, though without much success.

If Dash was at the ball tonight, she hoped they might slip away. A second kiss appealed to her . . . what was she thinking? The best thing she could do would be to avoid Lord Daniel Dashworth altogether!

the cheval glass and looked at her reflection, from the mirror-backed topknot on her head to the toes of her silver slippers. The dress had a modest neckline compared to most of Sasha's, but Anne hoped it proved anyway, though without much success.

It has was herself tonight, she hoped they might this away. Perhaps that appealed to her the evening? The best thing she could do would be to avoid Lord Daniel Heathworth altogether.

Chapter Four

Anne knew she ought to stay as far away from Dash as possible at the Cuthberts' ball. Yet the moment she and Sarah ascended the stairs to the reception rooms, Anne found herself on tiptoe, combing the crowd for his handsome face.

Sarah gave her a little jab. "Stop craning your neck like a chit at the fireworks, my dear. You are quite spoiling the elegance of your ensemble. Madame La Jolie would not approve of such fidgeting. What are you looking for?"

Anne tried to laugh off her behavior.

Sarah pressed her. "I can tell you are looking for someone. Perhaps that darling Dashworth?"

"Do not be a goose. I wanted to know how many people are here. It is as simple as that."

"Hmmmmm. I think you are dissembling, my dear. But I will allow you your little secrets, at least for the moment."

Lord Rossiter joined them and made a handsome bow to each. "Ladies, a very good evening to you."

Immediately others joined them, and the laughter and conversation flowed freely. Anne tried to look around discreetly for Dash—only to be sure she kept her distance, she told herself. He was generally one of the later arrivals.

When the music began, Lord Ingram solicited her hand for a set. On one of her turns, she caught sight of Dash standing beside a lovely young woman. Anne almost tripped, but caught herself in time. Nevertheless, her heart fluttered alarmingly. Who was that lovely young woman?

The next time her steps brought her around to the same view, both were gone. She tried to concentrate on the figures of the dance and to keep a smile on her face. But inside she felt unaccountably empty, as though someone had stolen the core of her being. Why? After all, Dash meant little to her, a fribble by his own definition. Someone Sarah had called a scamp, a handsome rogue. Someone who had been kind to Ursa.

Someone whose kisses she longed to experience again. And again.

When the set ended, she curtsied to Lord Ingram, who bowed and escorted her to the sidelines, directly to Dash and his lady friend. Anne tried very hard to straighten her shoulders and bring a genuine smile to her face, though her empty feeling had intensified, and she feared her internal turmoil might show in her eyes.

She spoke not a word while the other three greeted one another, the unknown lady obviously being an intimate of both gentlemen, a very beautiful and perfectly gowned companion.

After a few seconds, Dash reached for her hand. "Oh, please excuse my manners. Gloria, may I introduce Miss Anne Talcott? Miss Talcott, this is my sister, Lady Gloria. She has just arrived in town."

Anne felt sunshine flooding her soul, breaking out in bright rays of welcome relief. She curtsied deeply, feeling her empty core fill with radiance. "How very nice to meet you."

"Entirely my pleasure, Miss Talcott." Lady Gloria tilted her head and smiled at Anne.

Dash sent Anne a knowing glance and spoke to his sister. "Miss Talcott and I had a most refreshing jaunt a few hours ago. I found the views most especially stimulating. Were your feelings the same, Miss Talcott?"

His eyes twinkled impishly, and she knew exactly what he was talking about, however in the dark their companions were.

Anne hoped her warming cheeks would not be noticed. "The view of the city is magnificent."

"How very enigmatic you are, Dash!" Lady Gloria turned to Anne. "Might I impose upon you to accompany me to the ladies' retiring room? I fear I have a repair to make."

At Anne's nod, Lady Gloria excused them both from the gentlemen, then linked her arm through Anne's. When they reached the retiring room, Lady Gloria drew Anne to a sofa and leaned close, speaking in a whisper. "I have no repair at all to make, Miss Talcott. I merely wished to speak to you outside the hearing of that rascally brother of mine. I declare I have never seen him so taken with a female as he is with you. We arrived this afternoon and when Dash returned, he spoke of nothing but you. All through dinner he entertained us with tales of Miss Talcott."

Anne shook her head in astonishment. "He did?"

"He did! Over the turtle soup, he praised your clever conversation. Over the baked lobster in cream sauce, he lauded your lovely countenance. Over the braised celery and partridge, he praised your strength of character."

Anne giggled. "Over the sweets, he must have mentioned my dog."

"We heard all about Ursa and his banishment while we were in the carriage on the way here to the ball. Both Gilbert and I were rendered speechless by his single-minded zeal."

Anne's pulse grew more and more rapid but she kept her voice light. "Then I presume I owe you an apology for spoiling your reunion and your meal."

"Why, not at all. I brought you in here to offer you my most heartfelt support and enthusiasm. It is long past time when Dash should give up his foolish non-conformity and establish himself. All his lovely estate needs to thrive is his attention and the aptitude of a clever lady with the house and gardens."

Anne drew a deep breath, sorry to spoil her companion's rosy view of the future. "Lady Gloria, I fear you have come to an unwarranted conclusion. Your brother has been kind to me in my first visit to London. That is all. I am quite sure he never intended to . . ."

"Believe me, Miss Talcott, I know my brother very well. I also know all the signs that point to the loss of one's heart to another. If I were not so excessively thrilled by the situation, I would find his enthusiasm quite amusingly tedious. Sort of like a little boy with a new set of toy soldiers, if you will excuse the very poor analogy."

Anne had a sudden vision of Dash as a boy opening a new box of shiny soldiers. He must have been an adorable child, however mischievous. She shook her head and forced herself back to reality. "I assure you, Lady Gloria, you are quite mistaken. Your brother may be paying some attention to me, but I know he has no serious intentions."

"I am quite unconvinced, Miss Talcott. I think you are perfect for each other, and I shall do all I can to promote the match."

Anne opened her mouth to reply, but quickly snapped it shut. How could she tell this lovely lady that Dash was not at all the kind of man who appealed to her, that he was far too roguish, not nearly earnest enough?

Lady Gloria glanced around the nearly empty room, then leaned close and whispered. "You know, Miss Talcott, it is quite true what they say. Reformed rakes do make the best husbands."

Anne stifled her gasp and turned it into a smile. "Oh, I have heard so." She hoped her remark was sufficiently innocuous.

"I shall be guarding your interests, my dear. Now we should return before the gentlemen retire to the card room without us."

As they walked toward the ballroom, Dash hurried up and folded Anne's hand under his arm. " 'Scuse us, Gloria. I thought you'd never come out of there, and I need to speak with Miss Talcott."

Gloria grinned knowingly and gave Anne a little wink.

Dash led Anne away from his sister. "I saw you were dancing with Ingram. Now, I want to warn you about him. Fine fellow, one of my best friends and all that, but a bit of a loose screw. Definitely not the one for you, with your high standards. He is not a bad fellow, not immoral or wicked, but he has no ambitions yet, needs a bit more time before he is ready to settle down."

Like yourself? she wanted to ask, but held her tongue.

"And don't think about Barnett, either. Just the opposite, an old bore, prosy and dull. Cannot want that for you."

Before she realized where they were strolling, they had traversed the balcony and gone down the steps into the garden lit with colorful paper lanterns. The music from the ballroom still sounded softly in the background, combined with the occasional call of a far-off nightingale and the singing of insects.

Anne knew very well where he was heading. She both wanted them to get quickly to the darkest corner of the garden, and at the same time she wanted to slow down and extend the moment she knew would soon arrive. Her desire for more kisses easily overcame her hesitation, however, and she said nothing as he led her deeper into the velvety darkness. She shivered with the anticipation.

"Are you chilly, my dear?"

She shook her head, but he slipped out of his jacket anyway and placed it around her shoulders. She felt the warmth of his body envelop her and heard a fluttering sigh escape her lips.

He settled her on a stone bench and sat beside her, but his words were unforeseen. "Now that you have seen the Heath, are there other attractions and events we should put on our agenda to visit, Miss Talcott? I am in need of a program of improving activities such as you wish to have for yourself."

Though she had expected a more romantic topic, such as the beauty of the silver half-moon or the warmth of the breeze, Anne responded honestly. "I have long wished to see St. Paul's Cathedral. It is said to be the most magnificent of Sir Christopher Wren's creations."

Even in the faint light, she could see the dismay on his face and she laughed softly. "I presume you are not fond of cathedrals?"

"Perhaps my aversion results from my lack of familiarity with such places. As I said, many elements of my education are quite lacking."

She spoke in a teasing tone. "And in this case, you may wish to avoid correcting that deficiency?"

"You are merciful indeed, Miss Talcott."

"There are many other choices. The Tower of London. The Royal Academy's summer exhibition. The Egyptian Hall."

He nodded and she listed more of the sights she longed to see. "You have probably seen all these places many times."

"Hardly. I shall be honored to join you in such a program of improvements, and I suggest we start tomorrow."

She nodded, watching a cloud approach and slide across the half-moon. In the silence, she was certain he would lean closer and kiss her again. Her every nerve stretched tight and tingled, making her entire body sparkle inside, as if filled with a foaming champagne. She ran her tongue over her lips, closed her eyes, and waited.

He lifted her hand and loosened her glove, drawing it down her arm with teasing fingers. When he raised her wrist higher, she opened her eyes and watched as he touched his mouth to her palm, then to the sensitive inside of her wrist. The feeling was exquisite.

"Now, I must take you back to the ballroom, Miss Talcott, before someone misses us."

"But . . . but Dash—" Her voice sounded low and husky, unfamiliar to her own ears. Where were the kisses she yearned for?

"You have your very proper reputation to think of," he whispered. "Here."

He held out her glove and she plunged her hand into it, wiggling her fingers into place. Her throat felt tight and tears threatened to fill her eyes.

She had to hurry to catch him as he moved back toward the house. At the steps, he stopped and placed a little kiss on her forehead, then took back his coat and shrugged into it. "Miss Talcott, consider yourself very fortunate. You have been providentially rescued from a dreadful fate. I believe my sister was spying on us. She would be just the person to insist we wed if she caught us kissing."

Anne opened her mouth to speak, then stopped, her breath suddenly sucked out of her body. She had almost responded in a most improper way.

She had been about to ask what he found so inappropriate about marrying her.

Anne held herself ramrod straight and curved her lips in a smile. Hours remained before Sarah would be ready to leave, hours in which Anne must not give a hint of how flustered she felt. It was only her pride that hurt, she told herself. The thought of marrying Dash had never entered her mind before his sister talked of it. Marriage to *him*? Never!

She looked around the ballroom with what she hoped was a normal gaze, one that gave nothing away about the disquieted state of her mind. She held her hands tightly together to disguise their trembling and choked back the lump that filled her throat. Beside her, Dash joked with friends, obviously celebrating his clever escape from his sister's machinations.

The smile Anne gave Lord Fancourt as he approached was completely false, but he did not seem to notice, bowing low and requesting her to join him for the next set.

"Delighted." Anne tried to catch Dash's expression as she took Lord Fancourt's arm, but he had turned away just enough that she missed his face, though she heard his laughter. Carefree as always, oblivious to her feelings.

Luckily the music was familiar, the steps easy. She kept her smile bright as her thoughts tumbled back and forth.

What did it matter that Dash so abhorred marriage to her? He was the last man in London she would consider as a potential match. He was everything she loathed in a man, a self-important yet thoughtless fellow with a dreadful reputation as a rake and a rogue. As for morality, he did not know the meaning of the word.

At the proper moment, she took Lord Fancourt's hands and whirled around with considerable liveliness. As for Lady Gloria's nonsense about reformed rakes making the best husbands, Anne could see not the slightest hint that Dash had any intention of reforming.

And she wouldn't have wanted him anyway. Her entire reaction made no sense. Instead of feeling offended and forlorn, she should be celebrating her own escape, just like Dash was doing.

At the closing bars of the music, slightly breathless, she curtsied to Lord Fancourt. The figures changed and he led her into a new formation for the second country dance of the set.

"You are looking particularly pretty tonight, Miss Talcott. That color brings out the blue of your eyes."

"Why, Lord Fancourt, how very sweet of you to say so."

The chord beginning the second dance signaled the end of their conversation. *A good thing,* Anne thought. She had not a thought in her head beyond the joy in Dash's voice when he announced the failure of Lady Gloria's alleged plan.

As she went through the paces of the country dance, Anne began to understand her strange feelings as a sort of anger. *I do not want to marry Lord Daniel, but it is most provoking to realize he is so dead set against marrying me.*

Why was his attitude so offensive to her? She pondered the question as she kept smiling, performing each pattern of steps.

She did not understand her feelings. Not at all. But she must put them out of her head.

Tomorrow she would have not the slightest problem spending time with Dash. Their friendship was exactly as it should be, without any necessity of obligation on anyone's part. And she would be very careful never to put herself in the position of being available for his kiss. She had allowed her imagination to wander into dangerous territory under the influence of a new and pleasant experience. From now on, she knew the dangers and how to stay away from them.

Dash tapped his toe in time to the music and kept his gaze well away from the dancers.

He was definitely in the soup now, though it could have been much worse out there in the garden if he had not caught a whiff of his sister's favorite Parisian scent. He had been about to initiate Anne into several new kissing techniques, and he still felt the disappointment, right down to that restless tapping toe.

Ingram and the others blathered on, something about the new bridge about to open, but he paid no attention to their words. He had his own problems, for though he had escaped Gloria's devious clutches, he was stuck shepherding Anne around town. And he had been the one who suggested it. Obviously he had overdone the claret at dinner.

Not that he regretted his offer. But what the deuce, St. Paul's Cathedral? His own tastes ran more to an evening at Vauxhall. Now there was a happier thought.

Then had she not mentioned the theater once, particularly something about seeing Shakespeare performed? Any mention of the Bard brought dreary thoughts of his odious old tutor and stuffy lecture halls in Oxford.

She talked of that new picture gallery in the village of Dulwich. Sounded dull, all right. Extremely dull.

And Lord Elgin's Marbles. Dash thought the rocks must be in his head.

Why had he ever offered his escort? "Devil take it," Dash muttered to himself. *I am trapped. But I will never let Gloria trick me into the parson's mousetrap.*

And there was the damned dog to consider. Visits to him. Avoiding his overzealous protective instincts. The hours would stretch to fill every day.

This was serious stuff, a long way from the silly job he'd set for himself a few weeks ago, to loosen her up, to show Miss Talcott just what a good time she could have in London.

Anne was surprised when the butler said her father was waiting for her in the library. She hurried in, leaving her shawl and gloves on the pier table.

"Ah, Anne," Baron Talcott said as she entered the room. He was still dressed in evening clothes. "Have a seat, my dear. Would you like a bit of wine?"

"Thank you, Papa. I will have just a sip."

He poured out a half glass and handed it to her. "I learned tonight that I have been neglecting you. Or perhaps you have been neglecting me. Smithers says you are quite the toast of the *ton* these days."

Anne sipped the wine. "What nonsense they have told you."

"Then it is not true that you are often seen in company with Lord Daniel Dashworth?"

"He is sometimes my partner for country dances. And he frequently takes me to see Ursa, out in the country." She tried to keep her voice light, unconcerned.

"Don't know the fellow, but I knew his late father and I see his brother, the present duke. Are you fond of him?"

"He is all that is kind, Papa. He has agreed to accompany me to several sights I wish to see. The Elgin Marbles. Things like that."

"I thought Lady Easterly wanted you here to visit such places."

Anne tilted her head and shrugged. "Sarah and I spend a great deal of time together. But she has things to see to from time to time, Papa."

The baron continued his interrogation. "I assume the young man conducts himself with propriety."

"Quite." *Too much propriety tonight!*

"And I assume he has some property?"

He had never spoken of any, but Anne remembered his sister had mentioned an estate. "Yes, so I understand."

Her father stared into the fire for a moment. Anne was certain he was about to pronounce Dash a rakehell and wastrel, unfit for his daughter's company. The longer the baron paused, the harder her heart pounded and the more she felt that empty, let-down sense of helplessness.

After an endless moment, Baron Talcott sat up straight and stared her in the eye.

Anne nibbled at her lower lip, wishing she could think of anything to say that might prevent his forbidding her to see Dash again.

He reached for her hand. "I give you my blessings, my dear. And you may tell the young man when he is ready to speak to me, I look forward to saying the same to him."

Anne felt her jaw drop open. *Amazing!* She hesitated for a moment, then spoke the truth. "I do not think there will be such a moment, Father. I do not anticipate receiving his offer."

She jumped up and raced out of the room before a flood of tears overwhelmed her. Foolish as it seemed, her heart felt broken.

Chapter Five

Anne pinched her cheeks to bring them a bit more color while she waited for Dash to arrive. Today they had scheduled a visit to Bullock's Museum in the Egyptian Hall, a place she heard was full of wonderful curiosities. She walked over to the window and peered out, hoping to see his carriage nearing their doorstep. If she had to wait more than a few minutes, she would be back wallowing in irresolution, worrying and fussing without end.

For the last ten days, Anne had managed to control her wayward thoughts regarding Dash. No matter what his sister assumed or her father heard in his club, Dash had spoken the words himself. *A providential rescue from a dreadful fate.* Surely that was exactly how he regarded his escape from her!

Contrarily, Dash kept her too busy to refine upon her disorderly thoughts and emotions. Sometimes, late at night, she gave into frustrated weeping at the chaos she felt deep inside, the twists and turns of uncertainty about her feelings, not to mention his. Usually she was too tired to worry about whether she wanted to marry Dash—or why he did not want to marry her. It seemed the whole marriage issue had been imposed by his sister and her father. If it were not for that one little kiss, she would have laughed off the entire situation.

The kiss. Deep inside she treasured the memory. She felt a very warm regard for Dash, but she dared not let it show. Nor did she dare to think about her feelings for fear of where the thoughts might lead. Instead, she threw herself into activity after activity.

Almost every morning they had ridden out to take Ursa for a run. Though the dog had not attempted to pounce on Dash again, the two enjoyed a very tentative truce. Sometimes Anne almost giggled out loud at the hostile stares they exchanged, as if they were rascally boys itching for a fight.

Dash's impeccable manners and quick humor smoothed their way around the city, to one attraction after another. If he was bored or disinterested in anything, it never showed. Even in St. Paul's, he courteously pronounced the great dome a marvel. At the Royal Academy, he patiently stood by while she examined every picture on view. The tale of the ravens at the Tower of London had been one of his favorites as a child, and he seemed elated to have discovered it once more.

He even gave her his escort to a meeting of a new society for advancing education, and to her amazement, he made a handsome monetary gift to their cause.

Only when she was alone did her concerns and fears surface and demand her notice. At times like this, when she had nothing to do . . . Just then she saw Dash's team come up the street. With a quick sigh of relief at deferring another round of self-argumentation and vacillation, she trotted downstairs and met Dash at the door.

A quarter hour later, Dash stopped his curricle in front of the commanding entrance of the Egyptian Hall and motioned his tiger to the horses' heads.

Anne stared up at the imposing façade, so very different than the usual London building. "I assume the look of the building is authentically Egyptian?"

"I have never been to Egypt, but I have seen engravings of buildings that resemble this one. Perhaps one would say it is authentic in spirit if not in actual construction."

Inside, once he paid their admission, they found a considerable number of people inspecting the displays. The largest number crowded around the famous coach once belonging to Napoleon.

Anne stopped and stared for a moment. "Other than the imperial arms on the door and all the gold ornaments, it looks rather ordinary, do you not agree?"

Dash nodded. "And a bit top heavy. Though filled with all the luxuries an emperor would require."

She shivered. "An emperor responsible for thousands of deaths all over Europe. Let's move on. I am most interested in the curiosities associated with the voyages of Captain Cook. I read some of his accounts and find them fascinating."

They were almost alone once they left the carriage area.

Dash stopped in front of a plaster figure dressed in a grass skirt and a breastplate made of shells. "Now there is a weapon! A Samoan club."

"He looks very fierce. Cook found many of the islanders quite unfriendly."

They moved from exhibit to exhibit, studying artifacts from the *Endeavor*'s expedition to Tahiti and beyond. Anne was pleased to see that Dash read the labels with the same interest she felt.

After more than an hour among the Maori spears, plant specimens from Botany Bay, stuffed birds with colorful plumage, more plaster figures with ferocious painted faces and strange South Seas costumes, Anne sank onto a bench.

"I believe I have reached the point where further looking will be useless. I have seen all that I can absorb in one day."

Dash sat beside her. "I enjoy watching you inspect these curiosities, Miss Talcott. You have a inquisitive mind and an excellent imagination. I think you are quite suited for a life of great adventure."

"Me? Surely you are teasing again. Adventure is not likely to be in my future, my lord."

"Perhaps not a voyage to the Antipodes, but adventure nonetheless. Perhaps the adventure of love?"

Anne turned to face him. "Now I know you are teasing. As you are well aware, my adventures in love are nonexistent. You provided me with a little kiss, but beyond that my experiences have been minimal. Not that it is any business of yours." Even to herself, she sounded too prim. And impertinent as well.

But Dash took it with a smile. "I gather I have touched a sore point, so I will return to a more felicitous subject. Have you read the collection of elegies written to honor Captain Cook after his death?"

"Yes. They were printed in one of the books containing the accounts of his journeys. Very touching. He was a great man."

The next day, when Anne returned from riding with Ursa, the weather seemed to threaten their evening's jaunt to Vauxhall. The wind picked up all afternoon. Black clouds drifted over the city, darkening the sky. The air seemed heavy with the threat of rain.

Dash had been unconcerned. "This will blow over

well before evening, so your introduction to the pleasure gardens will not be spoiled. I am certain of it. Just as certain as I am that you will be enchanted by the place."

Anne did not give voice to her doubts about either the weather or Vauxhall but thanked him for the ride and the use of Dusty, the mare for which she had developed a true affection. "You are certain we should dress in evening clothes even though we need to cross the river in a boat?"

"Take my word for it. We shall choose only the boats that are accustomed to carrying royalty, my dear. You need worry about neither their cleanliness nor their safety. I cannot, however, guarantee you will not step in some stray horse droppings or into a mudpuddle if you do not watch your step."

"Oh, be off with you. Such silliness does not deserve my attention."

Dash bowed and left as she entered the house just as a few fat raindrops began to splash on the pavement.

By twilight, Anne did not know whether she should congratulate Dash on his correct predictions of the weather, which indeed had turned for the better, with only a very few clouds now in the sky, or tease him about his luck in guessing.

The lights of many flambeaux on the shore and in the boats glittered on the rippled surface of the river as their party rode across the Thames. Lord Rossiter accompanied Sarah, and Anne enjoyed the attentions of both Dash and his friend Lord Fancourt.

Colored lanterns lit the promenades, which passed under arches of flowers and vines. The orchestra was already playing, and the volume of the music increased as they approached the rotunda and its stage.

Anne knew she was staring about with wide eyes but

she could not help herself. Not only was the setting amazing, the people were equally worthy of study. Men and women of all kinds, in all sorts of dress, milled around near the stage, from the fashionable to the obviously impure.

Dash gave her a wide smile. "Do you like it here?"

Anne nodded her head. "It seems like an enchanted fairyland."

"Yes. Though by daylight, its illusions are gone and the enchantment is faded indeed. That is why we come after night falls."

"I love seeing the pavilion and the decorations like this. I can see where it might be very disappointing otherwise."

Dash excused himself to visit an adjoining box where his friend Lord Ingram sat with a jolly group.

While he was gone, Lord Fancourt sat down beside Anne. "Would you like to stroll about the paths, Miss Talcott? Perhaps you would like to see the grottos or the statue of Milton?"

Anne agreed. "Why, yes, that would be most pleasing. I would definitely like to see Milton."

She accompanied him toward the paths winding through the trees and shrubbery, where many couples strolled arm in arm. Sounds of nightingales singing mixed with distant melodies at the whim of the breeze. In moments they had left the well-populated areas behind. One couple ahead of them disappeared into the shrubbery, or so it appeared. Anne heard an occasional giggle from the private bowers along the way. This was the part of Vauxhall that Sarah spoke of, where little secret trysts were conducted and many kisses stolen.

"Where are we headed, Lord Fancourt?"

"These walks twist and turn, but I believe it is impossible to get lost. Eventually they all join up again."

"Oh, I see. Where is that statue of Milton?"

"Don't remember quite where, but it could be around the very next bend in the path."

Lord Fancourt steered her to the left and then took a turn to the right. Unlike Dash, she thought, he did not seem to be well provided with conversational skills.

They passed a bench set back into an alcove, though a couple engaging in a warm embrace were not entirely hidden from view. Anne heard a few whispers from behind another hedge. Just what did Lord Fancourt have in mind?

And why had she come? Did she want to experiment with kissing a man other than Dash? Would it feel different or much the same? She hardly knew Lord Fancourt, though she had danced with him at several balls and taken supper in his company a few times. She did not feel as comfortable as she did with Dash, either. She assumed Fancourt was an honorable gentleman. Or was he?

How would she have known, other than the fact he was a good friend of Dash's? Had Dash foisted her off on him, set up this little stroll so that he could remove himself even further from the danger of being discovered alone with her by his sister or someone else who might promote a scandal unless they immediately announced their betrothal?

Anne was beginning to think Lord Fancourt had indeed lost his way. It seemed they had been walking for a very long time and she had lost all sense of direction on the curving paths.

"Would you like to sit, Miss Talcott?"

"Yes, I think a little rest is exactly what I need. Do you think we are near that Milton statue yet?"

"Perhaps." He led her to a stone bench, again set into a deep cove carved out of the dark hedges. Little light filtered into the spot. And she found the bench very narrow. He placed his arm around her shoulders. "I hope you are not feeling chilled."

"No. Not at all. And I have my shawl." She rearranged its folds as a way of keeping her face turned away from him. Now that they had come so far along the walks, she realized her mistake. Girls who walked deeply into the darkness were virtually announcing their availability for a bit of kissing. Surely not more than that?

Lord Fancourt cleared his throat. "Are you comfortable? I fear this bench is rather hard."

She could feel the hesitation in his manner and hoped he would give up the idea of a stolen kiss.

"Perhaps we should start back . . ."

"Already?" Lord Fancourt reached over and tilted up her chin until she was forced to look into his face.

"Miss Talcott, I find you a most pleasing young lady. I wish . . ." He leaned forward and rather bumped his lips into hers. She shrank backward, but he pressed harder. She pressed her hands against his chest and pushed him back.

"My lord, you must not take advantage—"

A loud voice suddenly rang out in front of them on the path. "Here they are!" Dash grabbed Fancourt's arm and hauled him to his feet. The calmness of his voice belied the violence of his movements as he spoke to Sarah and Lord Rossiter, who were a few steps behind him. "They are sitting right here."

To Fan, Dash hissed softly, but with deep menace in his tone, "Enough of that!"

Anne stood quickly. "Why, Lord Daniel, were you worried about us?"

"Not in the slightest, Miss Talcott." He spoke in a soft growl, but she could hear the tension in his voice.

Lord Fancourt seemed unruffled. "We were just resting on the way to the Milton statue, Dash."

"You know damn well that is a crock, Fan. Milton is nowhere near this path."

Sarah's laughter rang out as she linked her arm through Anne's. "You are a sly puss, Anne. I never would have believed you would run off to the dark lanes on your very first visit to Vauxhall. Now hurry back with us or we shall miss the fireworks."

Anne took Sarah's arm, and the three men followed behind, an ominous silence and palpable sense of disapproval radiating from Dash. Anne hardly knew whether to feel relief she had been rescued from Lord Fancourt's inept kiss or to feel mortified that Dash had discovered her in such a position.

Of one thing she was sure. Fireworks never looked more beautiful than through a film of tears. By the final burst of sparks, she had regained some measure of composure. She refused absolutely to let Dash see the level of her embarrassment.

A supper of chicken and ham was served at their reserved table in a pillared pavilion decorated with garlands of blossoms perfuming the air and surrounded by shrubbery and tall cedars. Dash's disapproving glare lasted through the food and wine, and Anne's attempts to keep up her spirits began to flag as the night wore on.

At last Dash took out his watch and checked the hour. "It is nearly time to return home. I have arranged for my carriage to be at the gate so that we do not have to re-cross the river. Miss Talcott, if you will take my arm, I will endeavor to show you the Milton statue as we depart."

Anne moved to him slowly, giving him a tentative smile.

He was immune. "Come along, it is late and I do not wish to have the horses standing for long."

She practically had to run to keep up with his long stride. He said nothing, but his strong disapproval still showed in his every movement. His frown had only deepened as the evening wore on. Finally, he spoke. "You may be one of the silliest females it has ever been my misfortune to encounter, Miss Talcott."

The sharpness of his words spurred her to anger. "Silly indeed, Lord Daniel? It was not silly for me to allow you a kiss on Hampstead Heath? But it was silly of me to accompany your close friend on an evening walk at Vauxhall? I wish to know just how you define the word *silly*." Her voice was hard and she snatched her hand from beneath his arm.

He stopped abruptly and caught her elbow, pulling her to him. She looked up at him for a moment before he crushed his lips to hers, tasting and seeking, turning her blood to fire. Her legs melting beneath her, she sagged against him and kissed him back with every bit of fervor in her soul.

When at last they moved apart, he shook his head. "Anne, you stun me. I am . . . I do not understand you. I do not understand myself."

"Come, before the others catch up." She took his hand and pulled him forward.

She did not understand either. What did it all mean? His anger, his passion, his impulsive embrace. Her pounding pulse, her sense of unbidden desire, her yearning to feel his lips again the moment they had left hers.

They turned a corner and before them stood the statue of Milton.

Dash shrugged. "Just another poet sitting on his exalted throne. Are you satisfied now?"

Dash was glad he had ordered the bottles of champagne to be waiting for them in the carriage, for the ceremony of popping the corks and pouring the wine and raising toasts to one another occupied most of the ride home and prevented awkward breaks in the conversation.

He was so angry he wished he could call out Lord Fancourt. Except how could one do that to a lifelong friend? And for something as foolish as stealing a kiss from a naive girl . . . whatever Fan thought he was doing spiriting off a green miss like Anne . . . well, obviously Fan knew exactly what he was doing. That was precisely the problem.

Dash watched her for a moment, laughing as though nothing could have possibly been wrong. She certainly had been willing to saunter off into the dark with Fan. Had she gone there with him on purpose? Were they developing a *tendre* for one another? Then again, had she not said one of her purposes for being in London was to gain experience? Perhaps she might think his one kiss was not sufficient experience. But if she needed more kisses, he, Dash, ought to be the one to enhance her experience.

When he accompanied Anne to her door, he knew his voice still sounded curt. "I assume you enjoyed your evening at Vauxhall, Miss Talcott? I regret I will be unable to accompany you on our usual morning ride to Freddy's tomorrow. I have other business I must attend to. I will send you a note when it is convenient for me to take you there again."

He was strangely disappointed in her cool response.

"I quite understand, Lord Daniel. I thank you for your escort."

She was inside with the door shut before he could respond.

Lord Fancourt hurried into the taproom and peered through the thick smoke.

"Over here." Lord Julian pushed a tankard of ale toward Fan.

"We got him!" Fan spoke the instant he was seated.

"Excellent!" Julie rubbed his palms together.

"Tell us the whole story." Lord Ingram also wore a wide grin.

"It was perfect. Poor Miss Talcott was a bit put out, but I managed to get her alone in the darkness and plant her a kiss just as Dash found us. The timing was exquisite. He was mad as a hatter and twice as ludicrous. No doubt in my mind. He is gone on that girl."

"Then we shall all collect!"

The three friends joined hands in glee.

Dash stared out of the window of his bedchamber at the lightening sky. What a fine fix he had landed himself in! He, the carefree neck-or-nothing Dash, had fallen in love with the unlikeliest of young ladies. He had never given love a second thought in all his twenty-nine years. Just an invention of the poets.

Ha! If love did not exist, then why was he in a black fog now, feeling an ache he had never felt before and had no idea how to remedy? Yes, the pain was actually physical, though he was stumped about where in his body it resided.

She would laugh at him if he declared his feelings for her. She wanted a husband of upright morality and sober propriety, not qualities for which he was noted. But he truly believed he had changed.

Since he had known Anne, he found he almost enjoyed literary discussions and visiting local attractions. Moreover, he knew he would never want another female but her. No one else could have her charming curiosity, her quick wit, her sweet and earnest kiss.

How could he convince Anne of his sincerity? He had given up everything of his old life already. He had sent off his mistress long ago. He had foresworn every invitation to dice or cards. He had little opportunity to drink to excess anymore. He had taken his sister Gloria's advice and intended to assume the control of his estate. He contributed money to any cause Miss Talcott championed.

And he certainly had no time for his usual haunts—the cock rings or mills—now that he was embarked on Miss Talcott's program of improvements. No, there must be another way of convincing her, if only he could think of what it was.

He lost himself in dreams unlike any he had ever had before of repairing and adding on to the house on his estate, living there with Anne and even children. No, especially children, his and Anne's. A fair-headed boy or two and curly-topped angelic little girls. Instead of seeming like the worst of sentences for unspeakable crimes, this now seemed like the best of all futures.

He could think of no other route but to throw himself on her mercy. Weeks ago she had confided what she wanted in a husband, a respectable man of the highest character. If he was not that man, the only way he could become that man was with her assistance.

But would she listen to him ever again?

True, he had been angry with her for running off with Fan that way. But anger was no excuse for being rude.

Tomorrow he would have to start again, almost at the beginning. He would call on her and beg her pardon.

Dash could hardly believe the direction of his own thoughts. What strange behavior love could bring a man!

Chapter Six

The next morning, Anne felt as washed out as the weather. Ponderous dark clouds filled the sky and the air was thick with heavy mist whenever the sheets of rain let up.

She called Mary to her room and told her to begin packing for their return home later in the week. Until she collected Ursa and made her excuses to Sarah, she could not set a date for departure, but after experiencing the wrath of Dash last evening, Anne had no desire to remain in London.

She sat down at a table to write belated regrets to several hostesses whose invitations she had accepted for next week. Certainly by that time she would be well on her way back to Dalby.

Her future seemed dreary. She knew she could not marry Mr. Lambert. Not after spending so much time with Dash, experiencing the laughter and the spirited conversation. She would rather be a lifelong spinster, free to make her own entertainment rather than raise a passel of sober little Lamberts, one more serious than the next.

On her bed she piled several ball gowns, dresses she would probably never wear again, not at any events held in her village or even in the neighboring market town. How silly Miss Talcott would appear in her London finery among the home-sewn gowns in the environs of Dalby.

When she was summoned to the drawing room, she expected to find some of the literary ladies she had not seen for more than a week. Instead Dash's vivacious sister was seated in the drawing room.

"Lady Gloria!"

"Ah, Miss Talcott. Please excuse me for arriving so early, but I am excessively anxious to hear about your evening at Vauxhall. I wanted so much to come, but my dear Dolph cannot bear the place and Dash refused to let me join your party. Do say you loved it, the grand cascade, the singing, the illuminations."

When she stopped for a breath, Anne summoned her vocabulary of superlatives. "Indeed, the gardens are spectacular."

"And the fireworks. They are said to be the best, though I am sure I have little grounds for comparison. Ever since I was taken there as a young girl, well, I am assured there is no better display in town. Then the dark lanes! I am sure Dash must have shown you those." She grinned and nodded as if encouraging Anne to relate every detail of the evening.

Lady Gloria would not have been so eager, Anne thought, if she had known of the debacle. "Did Dash not tell you about it?"

"He said not a word. Went out rather early for him. Said he would be at the club later. You must tell me, Miss Talcott, though it is most improper for me to ask . . . no, I cannot. You will think me a hoyden indeed. But I must! Did Dash show you the dark lanes?"

"He took me to see the statue of Milton on our way to the carriage." That at least was a straightforward truth.

As Lady Gloria launched into another paean to the beauties and entertainments of Vauxhall, Anne thought about how she would miss Dash and his eager grin. Not that she had seen much of his sense of humor last evening.

"Oh, I am so sorry I have spoiled your morning. You must have had many things to do, Miss Talcott. And here I am running on again about every visit I have ever made to the Garden. I shall make my good-byes to you now and let you return to your interrupted activities. When Dash returns to the house, I will back him into a corner until he tells me all about last night." She started out the door, then turned back. "You know, it was the oddest thing. A man arrived while we were at breakfast with the strangest message. He said something about a dog that was missing. Dash did not seem concerned, but I wonder if it was some kind of a code. He is not up to some havey-cavey business, is he, Miss Talcott?"

"I would know nothing about that, Lady Gloria. And if Lord Daniel tells any tales about my visit to Vauxhall, I implore you to take it all with a grain of salt."

"Oh, how intriguing! Good-bye, Miss Talcott."

Anne was halfway up the staircase before the implications of Lady Gloria's statements penetrated her brain.

She stopped and clutched the banister, her heart flooding with panic. Could the message have been about Ursa? She knew of no other dog Dash might be concerned with.

Ursa missing? Where could he have gone? If he ran away, he could be anywhere.

Or he could have been stolen. If he was gone, she

would never be the same. Life without Ursa seemed utterly impossible.

Her pulse pounded with fear as she rushed up the remaining stairs and grabbed for a pelisse. Somehow she had to find her way to Freddy's, to learn if Ursa was really gone.

And where had Lady Gloria said Dash had gone? To his club? More likely to some race meet or a mill with his pack of useless friends. Of course he would not be around when she needed him. He cared not a fig for Ursa anyway, not that the dog had ever warmed to him, either.

Oh, the thought of Ursa dragged off by some thieves or losing his way among the villages and fields he hardly knew—the thought was more than she could bear.

Dash made another circuit of Freddy's fields, now soggy with the persistent rain. Where had the damned dog disappeared to, anyway? Freddy said he had fed him last night and left him in the stable, but this morning, the big black cur was nowhere to be seen.

Dash had come immediately upon receiving the message, though he had taken care to give a false story to his household. Servants' gossip got around town so fast, and the last thing he needed was for some footman of Lord Talcott's to hear the rumors.

Dash reined up and looked toward the distant hills. On a few of their rides, he and Anne had circled around to Hampstead Heath. Other times they headed south. Dogs like Ursa were not exactly rare, but many seemed to prize the beasts. He once heard Byron had such an animal, and the big black monsters were quite in fashion.

He was thoroughly soaked in one of the cloudbursts

and he supposed he would feel the effects soon enough. But he went on, trying the southern route. In the mist little looked familiar, and he wondered if he had lost his way. Perhaps if he gave Ajax his head, the horse would find his way back to the warm dry stable or at least find the road back to the city.

Through the mist Dash saw a bridge ahead over a now-rushing stream. It looked like the place they had stopped a few days ago, when that other dog had barked at Ursa and both had waded into the stream before Anne called Ursa back. At the time he had figured there might be a fight brewing, but as he thought about it, he wondered. Was the other dog just defending its territory? Or could it have been a female, perhaps a female Ursa might come back to woo?

He crossed the bridge and headed Ajax into the wood on the other side, just through the trees to a small farm. There, standing sentinel near a small shed, stood a huge black Newfoundland, almost surely Ursa.

Dash called out to the dog. Not a muscle moved.

"Ursa, nice fellow. Come on over here. Come, Ursa." The dog did not move.

He called again, at last reduced to shouting, "Come here, you wretched cur."

"Kin I help ye?" A man in oilskins approached Dash from the farmyard.

"I think that is my dog over there. Or rather, my friend's dog who has gone missing."

"Aye. That fella has been around quite a while. Payin' court to my Queenie. I be thinkin' she's in a family way by now. 'Spect he's tuckered out. Ye want me to tie a lead on 'im?"

"Yes, if you please. He's too blasted big to carry. He'll have to walk home."

As Dash went closer, Ursa turned his head and gave Dash the first nonhostile look of their acquaintance.

"Well, old fellow, I think we'd better get you home and dried off." He stepped closer, and Ursa neither growled nor bared his teeth. When the farmer handed him a coil of cord, Dash looped it around Ursa's neck. The dog apparently was too exhausted to be anything but docile.

"Come on, boy." To Dash's surprise the dog followed him without the necessity of tugging on the cord. He handed a guinea to the farmer and thanked him profusely.

All the way back to Freddy's, Ursa stayed submissively beside Ajax.

As he turned a corner into Freddy's yard, Dash heard a voice that sounded like Anne's, a voice full of tears. Her back was turned to him, but he could tell from her crumpled posture and bowed head she was distraught.

Dash reined up and unfastened Ursa. He watched as the dog trotted toward Anne, showing none of his usual exuberance upon spotting his mistress.

Anne stood in the rain, ineffectually trying to brush the tears from her cheeks as Mr. Eckford tried to explain how Ursa had disappeared.

"He was here yesterday, but somehow, overnight . . ."

A familiar little sound, more a snuffle than a bark, made Anne turn. "Ursa!"

She dropped to her knees in the mud and threw her arms around the dog. Ursa's hair was wet and matted with burrs and dirt, but she pressed her face to his head anyway. "Where have you been, you naughty fellow? Where have you been?"

"Visiting a lady friend, it seems." Dash, looking almost as wet as the dog, dismounted and tossed Ajax's reins to a stableboy.

"Did you find him, Dash? Oh, I thank you so very much! And you are soaked through. How did you know where to look?"

"I remembered that brown dog that barked so hard at us from the other side of the river a week or so ago. Miss Talcott, I do believe your Ursa is going to be a father."

A half hour later, rain still pelted the yard, but Dash had helped dry Ursa while Anne and Freddy hung their dripping outerwear near the fire in Eckford's comfortable kitchen. Ursa slept by the fire, only the rise and fall of his breaths showing he was something more than a furry hearth rug.

Again extending his apologies for allowing the dog to escape, Freddy left Anne and Dash alone, explaining he had paperwork to catch up on.

"I thought he would never leave," Dash whispered as the door closed.

Anne looked at him in surprise. "I thought he was your friend as well as an employee."

"That is true, but I do not particularly want him to witness our conversation."

"Why not? He has been most kind to me even in the face of my wailing."

"I wish to speak to you, Anne. I need to ask you a question."

She leaned forward when he used her Christian name, looking bewildered.

Dash summoned his courage and plunged ahead. "We have spent a goodly portion of the last few weeks in company with one another, riding on the heath with

Ursa and at a number of social occasions around the city. I am curious to know if you have been converted to my view of life—that those events one could call fun are far more rewarding in the end than the strictly improving ones."

Anne gave him a shy smile. "I have considered your view, but I suggest the choice is flawed in itself. One kind of activity is not necessarily more worthwhile than another, speaking theoretically. If one asks would you rather go to a ball than a scientific demonstration, no answer could be ascertained without more information. You might choose the ball, having assumed the music would be excellent, the company agreeable, and the food nourishing. I might choose the demonstration, assuming that the scientist is skilled, the subject matter of interest, and the results illuminating. You might go to the ball and find the music poor, few friends on hand, and the punch watery. I might find the scientist a charlatan, his experiment a hoax, and the results fraudulent."

Dash stood and applauded. "You are brilliant. Which puts me in a terrible dilemma."

"Why?"

He sat again and slid close to her on the sofa. "In your company, I have enjoyed many activities otherwise unusual for me. But my enjoyment depended upon you, not on the nature of the activity. When we are together, you make me see things through different eyes."

"That is true for me too, Dash. I can say exactly the same thing. I have enjoyed many of the balls only because I have spent time with you. I once thought we were opposites, Dash. You like the city better than the countryside. You prefer elegant balls while I favor literary discussions and museums. You like to play cards with your friends while I like to read in solitude."

Dash took both of her hands in his. "But we enjoy being together."

Anne smiled. "Oh, yes, that is true. Though another difference is that I talk too much while you are a man of action."

He gathered her into his arms. "My lady, if it is action you prefer, I shall accommodate you momentarily, as soon as I ask your assistance. Anne, more than anything, I wish to become the kind of man you could admire, though I realize I start with many impediments. How, I must inquire, can I begin this program of improvements? Can you help me? Will you marry me, Anne?"

She looked confused. "But you said that marriage was a terrible fate. You barely escaped your sister's plot."

"Oh, no. I was trying to rescue you. The first time from being tricked into marrying me. And again, the second time, I rescued you from Fan—a good man, but not right for you."

She nestled in his arms.

"In fact, Anne, no man is good enough for you, but I am better than most because I will vow to make you happy whether by attending a literary salon, investigating the latest collection of curiosities to come to town, or escorting you to a variety of parties. Can I ever be the man who meets all your qualities?"

Anne stared into his eyes. What madness had seized Lord Dashworth and caused him to declare his love for her? If only it were true, but was it possible? Something had caused him to lose his sense. Men like Dash who led a life of carefree pleasure did not change because of some female.

Or did they?

Perhaps she should not doubt the power of love to alter a man's beliefs and behavior.

"Dash, I have tried to deny my love for you. I was sure you had no feelings for me beyond friendship. I even thought your sister and my father must have windmills in their heads."

"Then you do love me? You will give me a chance? Even if I cannot become your ideal, I love you, and I will promise I will never stop trying to be the kind of man you desire."

Anne felt tears well into her eyes. She had no more words and hoped his had run out as well. "Dash?"

"Yes?"

"I am still waiting for your third kiss."

Without another word, he fulfilled her wish.

MARLOW'S
NEMESIS

Debbie Raleigh

Chapter One

She was an angel.

Negligently leaning against the wall of the ballroom, Lord Marlow watched his future bride twirl past with a faint smile.

Slender, elegant, with a cloud of golden hair and brilliant blue eyes, Miss Anna Dashell had been readily toasted as an Incomparable. To add to her perfection, she possessed a modest and biddable manner that boded well for her potential husband. This maiden would never harp at a man for preferring the gaming rooms to the dance floor, nor bitterly complain if he sought the pleasures of his club rather than prancing from one dull soiree to another. She would always be pleasant, undemanding, and mindful of her duties.

Ah yes, Marlow silently acknowledged, *what gentleman could ask for anything more?*

It did not occur to him that the maiden might not be willing to become his bride. And why should it?

Not only was he titled, wealthy, and in possession of a large estate in Surrey as well as a townhouse in Mayfair, he was also indecently blessed with classically handsome features and a lean, muscular frame.

There were, of course, those who might consider him

a trifle arrogant and rather self-indulgent. Even a few of the more prudish members of Society condemned him as a shameless rake.

All in all, however, he was by far the most sought after bachelor in England. What maiden of any sense would possibly turn him away?

Slightly turning his head, Marlow regarded the gentleman at his side. Sir Henry Hammonds offered a striking contrast to his own elegant appearance. A short, blunt-faced gentleman with little regard to fashion, Henry was a passionate horse breeder who rarely noticed anything as tedious as mere humans. Only the fact that Marlow owned a successful stud farm made him a bearable companion. And only just.

"Well?" he drawled as Miss Dashell was led from the dance floor by a dazzled young buck.

"Well what?"

Marlow rolled his eyes heavenward. He had specifically bullied his friend to this tedious affair so that he could catch a glimpse of the future Lady Marlow. Oddly, he had found he desired Henry's approval.

Perhaps it was because he never allowed himself to actually consider the notion of tying his life to another. Or perhaps because he knew less than nothing about innocent maidens. But he wished an unbiased, brutally honest opinion of the female he intended to make his wife.

"What is your assessment?" he prodded with a hint of impatience.

With a grunt, Henry cast a judicious glance over the angel in pale pink silk.

"She'll do, I suppose," he at last conceded, although there was a startling lack of enthusiasm. "Clear skin, hair has a nice gloss, shoulders square, neck well arched. Can't see her eyes."

Marlow choked upon a laugh. Trust Henry to consider a potential mate with the same attributes he would chose in a mare.

"They are what I believe the artists refer to as a cerulean blue."

"What the devil does it matter what color they are? Do they look unclouded? No hint of disease?"

Marlow struggled to contain his amusement. "None that I could detect."

"Hmmm . . . well, her limbs are long and graceful. Should think she would foal easy enough. Pity we can't determine how wide her hips are." He pursed his lips in a thoughtful manner. "Hips are very revealing in a maiden."

A wicked glint entered Marlow's black eyes, which were startlingly dramatic when combined with his fashionably pale skin and the soft, silver-blond curls.

"I would be happy to seek out any information you might believe should be required, Henry. However, I must warn you that the maiden may not be overly eager to have me measuring her hips."

Oblivious to the teasing note in Marlow's voice, his companion gave a knowing nod of his head. "Gun-shy, is she? Well, according to gossip, you have a rare talent for easing the most skittish of fillies. I shouldn't think it would take too much effort to have the maiden willing to reveal her hips and anything else you might have a hankering to measure once you set your mind to it."

Marlow's gaze slid back to the lovely Anna. It was surprisingly difficult to imagine removing that virginal pink gown to have a go at those hips. Or a go at anything else, for that matter.

Despite her beauty, she was simply not the type of maiden to make a man consider such delicious thoughts.

Perhaps it was that angelic perfection.

"Yes. The only problem is whether I truly desire to set my mind to it."

"Ah, thinking of bolting, are you?" There was more than a hint of relief in the gruff voice. "Can't blame you."

An unwitting frown touched Marlow's brows. No. Of course he was not thinking of bolting. For God's sake, he had just come to the decision this was the woman he should wed. Just because he did not have the hankering to rush over and muss that blond loveliness did not mean that they were not a suitable match. Indeed, it seemed utterly wise to choose a bride who did not inspire his lust. Far tidier.

"No, I shall not bolt. I made a vow to my mother that I would be wed before my thirtieth birthday. I have less than three months to keep my word."

"Dashed foolish vow, if you ask me."

"Perhaps, but unfortunately it is my duty as an earl to ensure the future of my title. Many would claim it is my most important duty."

A rather sly smile crossed the bluff countenance. "Ah . . . a stud for the sake of aristocracy."

Marlow suppressed a shudder. What was the point in being queasy? He had known his duty since he was in the cradle.

"Precisely."

Perhaps sensing a portion of Marlow's distaste, Henry offered a faint smile. "Ah well, worse things a gentleman could be forced to endure, I suppose."

Marlow lifted a broad shoulder. "No doubt."

There was a long pause as Henry returned his attention across the crowded dance floor. "And you believe that is the proper filly?"

Marlow shifted against the wall, smothering a yawn. "Why not?"

"You desire the truth?"

A brow, several shades darker than the pale blond hair, rose in question. "Would it matter if I said, no?"

"She is delicate," his companion pronounced in censorious tones.

"Delicate? Bloody hell, Henry, a maiden is supposed to be delicate. I have no desire for a hulking brute of a wife. They are dangerous enough when they are not capable of beating a man senseless."

Henry offered one of his famous grunts. An obvious indication of his displeasure. "'Tis not her frame, though she is a shade narrow through the chest. It is her . . . spirit I consider lacking. She has no bottom. No fire."

Marlow narrowed his gaze in irritation. Hell's teeth. There wasn't a gentleman in London who wasn't tumbling over his feet to gain Miss Dashell's attention. Why was his friend being so contrary? "You must be noddy if you believe any man desires fire in his wife."

Henry stubbornly folded his arms over his barrel chest. "You were the one to claim you are desiring an heir."

"That does not mean I wish a shrew for a wife."

"As a breeder, you should recognize the danger of weakening the bloodlines," Hammonds chided with a hint of censure in his eyes. Almost as if Marlow were considering offering his favorite stallion to a common nag. "If you desire strong, healthy foals, you should choose a mare such as that." The grisly head tilted toward a maiden standing near the edge of the dance floor. "A thoroughbred if I have ever seen one."

Impatiently Marlow turned to flick a glance over the

supposed thoroughbred. All nonchalance was rudely wrenched from his body as he jerked away from the wall and gave a choked cough. Or perhaps it was a gag.

Now he knew his friend was daft. No one, not even the most dense of gentlemen, could possibly believe Miss Charlotte Rowe, the Shrew of Surrey, a preferable choice to Miss Dashell.

"That? You truly have gone soft in the noodle, Henry."

"Why?" The bushy brows pulled together in genuine puzzlement. "Just look at those elegant lines and the proud tilt of her head. She ain't a filly who would shy at the slightest noise nor give up her heart before the end of her race. Good blood in that one."

Against his will, Marlow discovered his attention lingering upon the small, slender form currently attired in a shimmering blue silk. Unlike his angel, Charlie possessed unfashionably dark curls and cold gray eyes that always seemed to be judging and weighing a gentleman to his detriment. Even worse, there was nothing meek nor pleasing about her. He had encountered rabid dogs with better temperaments.

"Good blood?" he muttered in disdain. "The blood of Lucifer, you mean. If I were to search all of England, I could find no more aggravating, ill-tempered, sharp-tongued vixen. I would as soon slit my throat as make her my bride."

The bushy brows rose in surprise at Marlow's vehement tone. "I presume the two of you are acquainted?"

"She is my neighbor in Surrey."

"Ah. Childhood sweethearts."

Marlow flinched in horror. "Hardly. Over the years Miss Rowe has pulled my hair, ruined my favorite pair of riding boots, blackened my eye, and shoved me into a midden heap," he growled, perhaps unfairly leaving out the fact that he might have on occasion deliberately provoked her ready temper. "I have come to the inevitable conclusion she is a raving lunatic."

Henry offered a traitorous shrug, not at all shocked by the decidedly unbecoming habits of Miss Rowe. "A spirited lass."

"A menace."

"A maiden who would give a man children he could claim with pride."

A most uncomfortable tightness flared through his stomach. He could almost see Charlie heavy with child. Charlie in the arms of her husband, those raven curls tangled and her porcelain skin flushed with passion . . .

Absurdly, the image rose with ready ease, almost as if it had been in his thoughts more than once. Far easier than that of his angel.

He gave an annoyed shake of his head. *Blast it all.* Charlie was a shrew. An aging spinster. The bane of his existence.

"Enough, Henry," Marlow snapped. "I have made my choice. Miss Dashell will soon become the next Lady Marlow."

"A pity." The man gave a shrug. "I should have placed my bet upon Miss Rowe."

Miss Charlotte Rowe chewed her lip in fury.

She had taken such care. For weeks she had scoured the ballrooms and assemblies of London. She had attended the theater, sat through ghastly poetry readings, visited museums, and forced herself to make the polite rounds of afternoon calls. She had even braved the horrors of Almack's, all to discover the perfect maiden.

And at last she had. Miss Dashell was everything she could desire for her young, sensitive brother.

Not only was she beautiful and well bred, but she possessed a quiet, modest nature that was quite pleasing. Never had Charlie noted the maiden tossing a petulant tantrum or demanding that others bow to her whims. She had never even been known to speak in anything over a bashful whisper.

Perfect for Tom, who, quite frankly, was terrified of women.

But now . . . after all her tedious effort, all the hours she had sacrificed, her well-laid schemes were being threatened in the most unexpected, most unpleasant manner.

Marlow.

Her jaws nearly cracked as she glared at the tall, fair-haired gentleman who hovered solicitously about Miss Dashell. What the devil was the arrogant toad doing? He had never before revealed an interest in debutantes. In truth, he was notorious in his blighting condemnation of innocent maidens and their marriage-mad mamas.

But there could be no denying that over the past week Marlow had developed a suspicious habit of making an appearance at even the most dull affairs. With the most correct manners, he would lead Miss Dashell onto the dance floor and then remain only long enough to exchange a few polite pleasantries with the maiden before disappearing to his usual haunts. He had even been seen to be driving her in the park, an unheard-of occurrence for the most notorious rake in London.

If she did not know better, she would presume that he was courting the maiden. But that was absurd.

"Good heavens, Charlie, do you have the grippe?"

With a tiny jump of surprise at being so rudely

wrenched from her dark thoughts, Charlie turned to regard a prettily plump maiden with a halo of reddish blond ringlets.

"I am sorry, Margaret, what did you say?"

The shrewd pale eyes studied her with a curious interest. "You have been standing in this corner with your face puckered in a sour expression for the past half hour. Whatever is the matter?"

"It is that arrogant devil," she readily confessed.

The pale brows rose in mild puzzlement. "You have just described most of the gentlemen in London. Which particular devil are you referring to?"

"Marlow."

"Ah." Margaret shifted her attention to the elegant, indecently handsome gentleman. "Now he is a delicious devil."

"Margaret."

"What?" The maiden lifted her hands in a helpless motion. "Is it my fault that he possesses the face of an angel and the form of a Grecian statue?"

Charlie clenched her teeth. "He also possesses an evil temper, a stunning determination to always have his own way, and a habit of treating others with utter disregard."

The words came out with rather more force than Charlie had intended, and it was no surprise when her friend gave a startled laugh.

"A rather scathing condemnation. Just how well are you acquainted with Lord Marlow?"

How well? Sweet saints. She knew that he rose at dawn to ride even on the dampest mornings, that his favorite food was raw oysters, and that he detested mushrooms. She knew that he sulked when his will was crossed, and yet could laugh at himself. He was devoted to his mother and respected his father in a distant manner. He was charming, vain, and at times frighteningly ruthless. He was also, she grudgingly conceded, quite without pretensions and excessively generous when it came to tenants and his family retainers.

Having been raised practically in one another's pockets, it was impossible not to be intimately acquainted. Intimately acquainted enough to drive each other batty.

"I know Marlow well enough to know he has never before professed an interest in debutantes. Indeed, he has often referred to them as the greatest plague ever to have infested London."

"Ah well, most gentlemen protest their fervent distaste for debutantes until the proper maiden manages to ensnare his heart," Margaret retorted with a philosophical shrug. "Obviously Lord Marlow has been smitten."

"Smitten." Charlie offered a snort of disbelief. "Fah."

"Why such disbelief? As difficult as it might be to admit, Miss Dashell has taken London by storm. There has yet to be any gentleman immune to her charm."

"Not Marlow." Charlie slowly turned her head to regard the gentleman as he leaned down to catch the soft voice of Miss Dashell. An uncomfortable pang twisted her stomach. "It is not possible."

Chapter Two

At precisely three o'clock, Lord Marlow stood within the Dashells' large marble foyer. He was appropriately attired in a fitted blue coat with a dove gray waistcoat only modestly embroidered with silver threads. His cravat was neatly, but not extravagantly, tied. His diamond stickpin was a statement of wealth without pretensions, and his silver-blond curls were artfully brushed toward his lean countenance.

And in his fingers was clutched the large bouquet of pink tulips that his valet had warned were de rigueur for calling upon an innocent maiden.

He felt a perfect nitwit.

It was no wonder that gentlemen of sense avoided this courting business, he grimly acknowledged. Never did he believe he would join the horde of buffoons who pranced and paraded before a maiden to attract her giggling interest. Hell's teeth, might as well be a dancing bear.

At least he had the satisfaction of knowing that none of his friends were about to take note of his foolishness, he reassured himself, impatiently awaiting the return of the sour-faced butler. They would all be comfortably settled in their clubs, or more likely still sleeping off the effects of their pleasure-drenched evening.

Shifting uncomfortably, Marlow heaved a sigh of relief at the sound of approaching footsteps. The sooner he was done with this ridiculous business, the better.

The precipitate relief, however, was short-lived.

Rather than the starchy butler he was expecting, a slender maiden with familiar raven curls and aggravatingly beautiful features stepped into the foyer. He stiffened in prickly embarrassment as her cool gray eyes flicked over his elegant form and the flowers he so ridiculous clutched in his hands.

Damn and blast.

Of all the people he did not wish to see at this moment, it was Charlotte Rowe.

The feeling seemed to be entirely mutual, as the maiden planted her hands upon her hips and stabbed him with an accusing stare. "You," she breathed in low tones.

With an effort, Marlow swiftly gathered his composure. He was not about to allow this vixen to realize the extent of his discomfort. She possessed too many weapons as it was. "As astonishingly clever as always, Charlie," he drawled in that tone he knew set her teeth upon edge. "Yes, it is I. I trust you are well?"

A hint of annoyed color stained the pure alabaster of her skin. "Quite well."

"And your mother and Tom?"

She frowned in impatience at his determinedly polite tones. Clearly she was spoiling for an argument. Hardly surprising. She was always spoiling for an argument. "They are, of course, well."

He slowly arched a brow. "There is no 'of course' about it. I have it on excellent authority from my mother that there is a dreadful chance of obtaining a chill in such damp weather and that several of her acquaintances have taken to their beds out of fear of the uncommonly thick air."

Since they were both aware that his mother was prone to delighting in ailments in both herself and others, Charlie was naturally unimpressed with his worrisome comments.

"Marlow, what are you doing here?" she sharply demanded.

He clutched the flowers, feeling as if his cravat was suddenly choking him. His expression, however, remained set in lines of mocking amusement. "Good heavens, perhaps you are not as clever as I have just claimed, Charlie. Surely any creature of sense could comprehend the obvious reason a gentleman would be arriving at a young maiden's home properly armed with flowers and the prerequisite bemused expression."

"You are here to court Miss Dashell?"

"Yes."

Her brows drew together in an ominous manner. "Why?"

He gave a sharp, humorless laugh. "Since when have I been bound to share with you the intimate secrets of my heart?"

"Heart? You have never been bothered with such a troublesome organ," she charged, with an edge to her voice. "Which makes me curious as to why you would be willing to risk appearing the buffoon."

Marlow's nose flared as her insult slid easily home. She would have to know he would indeed feel the fool. And that he would as soon be swinging from the gallows as to playing the besotted lover.

The fact that she deliberately thrust her barb into his

most vulnerable spot only stirred the flames of his rising temper.

"A buffoon?" His smile was thin. "I will have you know that I appear the perfect suitor. Not that I would expect you to recognize such a rare beast. I have warned you for years that your shrill tongue would put off the most desperate of gentlemen."

Her ludicrously long lashes briefly fluttered at his precise insult, but with the courage that he had always grudgingly admired, she stood her ground firmly.

"You desire to wed Miss Dashell?"

He shrugged. "Why not?"

"For one thing, she is barely out of the nursery."

His lips tightened. He would not allow her to make him feel the lecherous rogue on top of a buffoon.

"I prefer younger maidens." He deliberately allowed his gaze to freely roam her slender form, quite prepared to follow her lead and hit below the belt. No one could aggravate him like this woman. No one. "When a female is left upon the shelf for too long, she is bound to become wrinkled and more than slightly bitter."

She did not even flinch. "Ah yes, far more pleasurable to chose a child who is too frightened to do more than nod in agreement."

Ignoring the fragility of the tulips, Marlow crossed his arms over his chest. "You are hardly flattering of Miss Dashell. Could it be that you are envious, Charlie?"

"Do not be absurd."

"It would not be surprising," he pointed out with a taunting smile. "She has captivated every male in London. It must be difficult for those less fortunate maidens."

He might have known his arrow would be far off the mark. To her credit, Charlie had never been particularly vain. In truth, he had often wondered if she ever realized just how truly lovely she was. Well, as long as she kept that pert mouth shut, he was swift to add.

"I am far from being envious, Marlow," she retorted in tight tones. "I happen to hold Miss Dashell in great esteem and have hopes that she will be fortunate enough to chose a husband who will treat her with the gentle kindness that she obviously is accustomed to receiving."

A faint suspicion bloomed in his heart. Until this moment he had been too angrily embarrassed at being caught acting the ridiculous suitor to consider Charlie's interest in Miss Dashell. Now he could only wonder at her odd behavior. "Such consideration for a maiden you are barely acquainted with, my dear," he said slowly, his eyes narrowing. "Do you take such an interest in all debutantes and their prospective husbands?"

"I . . . have come to care for Miss Dashell."

If Marlow was not so well acquainted with this maiden, he might very well have missed the revealing manner in which her tongue touched the edge of her mouth. As it was, he knew immediately that she was up to something nefarious. "That is rather odd."

"I cannot imagine why," she swiftly retorted.

He took a step toward her tense form. "Because you have always preferred those females who share your own bluestocking tendencies—something Miss Dashell most certainly does not."

"Perhaps I hope to reform her."

"Hardly likely, when she shall be wed before the end of the Season."

The gray eyes sparked with annoyance at his tenacious probing. "There are some gentlemen who prefer a wife who possesses an independent spirit and love for learning."

Marlow might have pointed out there were also some

gentlemen who enjoyed leaping from buildings just to see if they could do so without breaking their neck. Instead he concentrated upon what this devious woman was attempting to conceal from him. "Do you speak of a specific gentleman?"

Her sudden jump gave her away. "What?"

"Ah ha." A smug smile curved his lips. "That is it."

Charlie gave a shrug but she could not entirely hide her growing discomfort. "What on earth are you babbling about, Marlow?"

"It is Tom, is it not?"

Her tongue once again peeked out, oddly making Marlow aware of just how full her lips were when they were not pinched into a sour frown. Full and soft and a delightful shade of pink. Surely they begged for a man's kiss?

With a sudden flare of shock Marlow realized that a familiar, slow heat was beginning to ignite within him. He shifted uncomfortably.

"Tom?" she was saying with a poor imitation at innocence.

Marlow ruthlessly returned his thoughts to the matters at hand. "You hope to lure that girl into wedding your hapless brother."

The mere hint of censure toward her beloved brother brought a militant glitter to the gray eyes. Charlie had always been revoltingly overprotective of her younger sibling, which Marlow was quite certain explained Tom's vague, utterly self-absorbed character. It had been a source of contention between them for years.

Or at least one of many contentions, he wryly corrected. The others had included her nitwitted refusal to accept the most sound advice, her relentless condemnation of his hedonistic pleasures, and her utter refusal to surrender to his male authority.

Of course, this seething contention had not always been quite so fierce. With two such strong wills their relationship was bound to be stormy, but there had been a great deal of friendship during their youth. There had even been times when he had thought he could never have another understand him so completely.

It was not until he had returned from school upon his eighteenth birthday that the battle lines had been so firmly established. Oddly, he could remember the exact moment as if it were seared onto his mind.

He had been anxious to find Charlie and brag of his newfound independence. It had taken him some time to at last track her to a distant hayloft, where she was fussing over a litter of stray kittens. After nearly a year since he had last seen her, Marlow had discovered himself caught off guard by the decided changes that had occurred. The playmate of his youth had abruptly been replaced by a young maiden of stunning loveliness. He could still recall the shock and discomforting awareness that had rushed through him. She had been seated in the dusky shadows, her gown disheveled to reveal a startling amount of her delicate curves, and her curls tumbled about her perfect features.

Perhaps he should have turned away when he realized what was occurring. Instead he had walked forward and simply gathered her into his arms as if he had been waiting for that moment his entire life.

A grimace touched Marlow's features at his outrageous stupidity. It did not matter now that she had so sweetly melted against his stirring body. Or that she had been the one to pull them both back into the soft hay. Or even that it was he who had at last come to his senses and brought an end to the near disastrous encounter.

From that moment on, he had become the enemy in Charlie's mind. And nothing was about to change that now.

"There is nothing the matter with Tom," she reluctantly retorted, thankfully unaware of his inner thoughts. "He happens to be a very kind and tenderhearted gentleman. He would make any woman a fine husband."

Marlow gave a snort of disgust. "Fah. He would make any maiden miserable."

"How dare you." She gritted.

A dangerous prickle entered the air. It was the same prickle that occurred just before she had pulled his hair and blackened his eye and thrust him into the midden heap. He eyed her warily.

"Charlie, we both know that Tom doesn't possess the least interest in anything beyond his ridiculous determination to become the next Michelangelo. Would you condemn Miss Dashell to a marriage with a gentleman who would barely acknowledge her existence, let alone indulge her love for Society?"

She at least possessed the grace to blush at the truth in his accusation, although her expression remained grimly stubborn. "Oh, and I suppose you intend to put off your male pursuits so that you can constantly squire your wife about town?"

Marlow was unprepared for her sharp attack.

It had been difficult enough to force himself to the point of selecting a maiden for a wife. He was not at all ready to consider what would happen to his delightful existence once he actually said "I do."

"That is between Miss Dashell and myself," he informed her in arrogant tones.

"Not if I have anything to say about it," she warned.

"Ah, but fortunately you don't."

Mutiny flashed in her eyes as she gave a flip of her head and marched toward the door. "We shall see."

The clear challenge was too much for any gentleman to bear. Moving before he could even consider what he was doing, Marlow reached out to firmly grasp her with one long arm. Employing the easiest of jerks, he hauled her next to his wide chest. "Charlie, do not stand in my way unless you wish to be hurt," he warned softly.

Her eyes widened and a startling color filled her cheeks at his intimate hold upon her. Still, she did not swoon, nor even slap his face, as she no doubt had every right to do. Instead she deliberately lifted her foot and stomped painfully upon his toes.

"Your threats do not frighten me, Marlow," she growled.

He glared down at the countenance that was only made more beautiful by her vibrant anger. It had been years since he had held her so closely, but oddly he was able to recall that precise scent of practical soap and honeysuckle, and the unfortunately delicious manner her body fit so exquisitely to his own. He was also aware that he was reacting with that same frightening rush of need that had nearly undone him years ago.

Foolishly, however, he did not thrust her away as he should. He did not even attempt to battle the sudden heat flowing through his blood. It would be a worthless effort. His arm tightened as he offered his own challenge. "I never lose, especially not when it comes to matters of the fairer sex, my ill-tempered shrew. I suggest you chose another maiden for your brother. Preferably one who has no wits and little hope for marriage to another."

Her breath hissed through her teeth. "Odious beast."

"Vixen."

"Toad."

"Baggage."

"Rotten, loathsome, wicked . . ."

The admirably descriptive insult was brought to a sudden halt as a loud cough echoed through the foyer. Together Marlow and his captive turned their heads to discover an elderly butler regarding them with a frown that could curdle milk.

"Pardon me, my lord, but Miss Dashell is prepared to receive you now."

Chapter Three

Marlow battled his way through the crowded ballroom with a distinct sense of impatience.

He did not wish to be at this dismal affair. Not when he had been invited to any number of gatherings that all promised to be vastly more entertaining than this collection of dragon dowagers and giggling debutantes.

Unfortunately, Miss Dashell was bound to attend. And until he could be certain that she was set upon becoming his wife, he was still bound to play his foolish role of devoted suitor.

A flare of anger threatened to rise, only to be sternly smothered as he thrust his way past a gaggle of fussily attired bucks. It was not entirely Miss Dashell's fault that she continued to waver.

After his confrontation with Charlie in the foyer two days ago, he had been out of sorts and not at all capable of pretending a suitably besotted manner once he had been in the company of Miss Dashell. In truth, he had barely taken note of the timid maiden during the prerequisite twenty minutes, and had left still carrying the tulips he had brought for her.

Dodging a large matron who threatened to tread on his toes, still sore from Charlie's vicious attack, Marlow at last spotted his fair-haired angel. His features hardened in determination as he plotted a direct path to her side. He wanted to be done with his obligatory dance so that he could flee the smothering heat and chattering din.

It was enough to drive any reasonable man dotty.

With his narrowed gaze trained upon Miss Dashell, he was already stepping to her side before he belatedly felt a tingle of awareness shiver over his skin. Reluctantly turning his head, he met the glittering glare of Charlie, who was already comfortably ensconced next to the maiden.

A shock of something perilously close to pleasure raced through him before Marlow sternly forced himself to wrench his attention away.

No. He had allowed the vixen to ruin his last encounter with his future wife. She would not be allowed to do so again.

Taking Miss Dashell's hand, he lightly raised her fingers to his lips, gazing deep into her eyes in a manner that sent any female's pulse racing. "Good evening, Miss Dashell. May I be bold enough to say you are in remarkable beauty this fine evening?"

An enchanting blush touched the creamy cheeks. "Thank you, my lord. Have you been introduced to Miss Rowe?"

His smile thinned as he was forced to include Charlie into their conversation. "Actually, Miss Rowe and I have known one another since the cradle."

"Indeed we have." Charlie met his gaze with a challenging expression. "And I must say that I am decidedly surprised by your appearance at such a tepid affair, Marlow." She cast a coy smile toward the younger maiden. "I fear Lord Marlow has always possessed a violent dislike for polite Society. He far prefers his clubs and the gaming hells that so fascinate some gentlemen."

Miss Dashell batted her long lashes. "Oh?"

He ground his teeth. Someday . . .

"I will admit too many gatherings are dull business, but how could any affair be tepid with Miss Dashell present? She is a rare treasure among the unfortunate dross."

"And you would know all there is to know about the dross, would you not?" Charlie sweetly inquired.

Marlow took a half step toward the unruly wench before sternly collecting himself. He could not lose his temper. Not before the woman he hoped to lure into marriage.

Somehow replacing his smile, he tenderly regarded the sweet features that were a sharp contrast to Charlie's vivid, passionate countenance.

"Tell me, Miss Dashell, are you to attend Mrs. Carter's charming al fresco on the morrow?"

She offered a shy shake of her head. "I fear not. Miss Rowe has been kind enough to invite me to join her family on an excursion to Wimbledon for the day."

"Indeed?" His hands clenched. "How lovely."

Miss Dashell smiled, utterly indifferent to the dangerous glitter in his eyes. "Yes, I am quite looking forward to our time together. Miss Rowe is so clever and charming."

"Oh yes, she is very clever." Marlow sensed Charlie give a small shift of her feet. She at least could perceive his growingly dangerous mood. "But we cannot have her monopolizing your days. There are far too many of us poor souls longing for a measure of your attention."

"Oh my lord." Miss Dashell dipped her head in seemingly embarrassment. "You always say the most charming things."

"Rot," Charlie muttered in barely audible tones.

He flashed her a cold glance. "Is something the matter, Miss Rowe?"

"Pardon me." Her smile was patently false. "There was a vile odor in the air."

Deliberately he reached out to take Miss Dashell's hands in his own, turning her toward him to create at least the illusion of privacy. "Since you have denied me your companionship tomorrow, my dear, I do hope you will find it in your heart to promise to join me in my theater box on Friday. There is to be a particularly amusing farce."

"Is there? I suppose . . ."

"A farce?" With grim determination, Charlie insinuated her way between Marlow and his companion, firmly entwining her arm with that of Miss Dashell. "But how delightful. I particularly enjoy a good farce, as does Tom, of course."

"I do not recall you possessing a taste for farces, Miss Rowe," he snapped in annoyance.

"No? Perhaps you have merely forgotten. There is nothing I adore more."

Marlow knew what he would adore at that moment. Unfortunately there was no way to bundle Charlie over his shoulder and toss her out the door without creating a rather unpleasant scene.

Enjoying the image of having the minx firmly in his control, Marlow failed to head off trouble before Miss Dashell was already laying her hand upon his arm with a pleading smile.

"Would it not be delightful to have Miss Rowe and her brother join us, my lord?" she said in those soft tones.

"Join us?"

"Well, I know so few people in London. It is a comfort to be assured of a few familiar faces."

"Of course." Marlow silently cursed his uncommon stupidity. He was a master of seduction. A gentleman who had lured and charmed women for years. And now, because of one aggravating female, he was bumbling about as if he were the veriest greenhorn. Turning his head, he stabbed his nemesis with a lethal glare. "Miss Rowe, I do hope you and your brother will consent to join us?"

She did not even bother to hide her triumph. "What a very charming notion, Marlow. We would be delighted."

"Lovely." Marlow abruptly held out his arm. There was at least one place in this godforsaken crowd where he could rid himself of Charlie and her vexing interruptions. "Miss Dashell, I believe this is our dance."

Charlie smiled with more than a hint of satisfaction as she left the retiring room and moved down the empty hallway. By now Marlow should have finished his dance with Miss Dashell and would be forced to politely bow and move away. Which meant that she would have the remainder of the evening to continue her subtle persuasion of Tom's gentle charms. A persuasion she was quite certain was coming along quite nicely despite Marlow's persistent pursuit.

Not that her smile was entirely at the thought of winning the maiden for her sensitive brother, she ruefully conceded.

However childish it might be, she could not deny that she took a great delight in besting the aggravating man. He was so arrogant, so utterly confident in his wiles that any female of sense would feel the need to tumble him from his own shining pedestal.

And she had bested him this evening, she acknowledged smugly. Not only would Miss Dashell be spending the entire day with Tom tomorrow, now she would have his company at the theater Friday evening. Even Marlow would have to admit that she had managed matters in a tidy fashion.

At least he would once he recovered his ready temper.

Oblivious to the fact that her steps had slowed as she silently gloated, Charlie moved past a darkened salon only to cry out in alarm when a muscular arm reached out of the shadows and plucked her through the open doorway. In the blink of an eye she was being firmly pressed to the wall by a threatening male form.

Just for a moment fear clutched at her heart. She had never heard of a poor maiden being attacked in the midst of a ball, but there was no denying the overly intimate press of the hard form and the arms that blocked any hope of escape. Then, slowly lifting her head, she encountered a pair of flashing black eyes and she hissed in exasperation. "Marlow, what the devil are you doing? You nearly gave me heart failure."

Not at all repentant, he continued to stare down at her pale countenance; an odd stillness settled about him. "I desired to commend your clever skill, my sweet. I am uncertain I have ever been so neatly outmaneuvered."

Although her initial fear had shifted to annoyance, Charlie felt a peculiar chill steal down her spine. There was a smoldering gleam in those eyes that she did not entirely trust.

"You were the one to teach me how to play chess, Marlow," she forced herself to retort. "You insisted only the boldest moves would win the day."

Astonishingly, he moved even closer—close enough

she could feel the hardness of his thighs through the thin silk of her gown.

"So I did," he murmured. "A lamentable mistake I now perceive. However, I recall that I also taught you never to deliberately place yourself in harm's way."

Charlie struggled to concentrate upon his words. Not an easy task when the heat of him was searing deep into her skin. "You seek to harm me?"

"I seek to have my way."

"Hardly surprising. You always seek to have your way."

"Ah, Charlie." Rather than revealing the anger that she sensed flamed just below the surface, Marlow offered her a dangerous smile as he lifted a hand from the wall and allowed his fingers to drift lightly over her bare shoulder. Charlie stiffened in shock, her breath catching as those fingers continued to trace an aimless pattern over her shivering skin, heading ever lower. "What am I to do with you?"

Charlie gave a choked sound as the fingers reached the low cut of her bodice. "Marlow."

"Yes?"

"What . . . what are you doing?"

His fair head lowered until his forehead was pressed to her own, his breath sweetly brushing her flushed skin.

"I am seeking to determine if your skin is still as tantalizingly soft as I recall."

Unbidden memories of the last occasion that Marlow had held and caressed her threatened to rise to mind. Memories of the searing kisses and perilous magic of his touch. Memories of how she had so desperately clung to him and moaned in pleasure. Memories of how she had begged him not to stop when he had pulled away.

Humiliating, embarrassing memories that she had

promised herself that she would never, ever allow to return.

She sucked in a deep breath and then wished that she hadn't. The movement only allowed him greater access to the soft curve of her bosom.

"Of course it is not," she snapped, wincing as her voice came out breathless and not nearly as steady as she would desire. "I am a wrinkled, bitter spinster upon the shelf, as you were so swift to point out."

"Ah." He shifted his head so that he could brush his lips over her temple, laughing softly as Charlie gave a violent jump. "Did I strike a nerve, Charlie?"

"Certainly not. Why should . . ." Her brave words were undone as she gave an inelegant squawk. His fingers had abruptly shifted to boldly slip beneath her bodice. "Marlow."

His lips skimmed to hover next to her ear. "I was mistaken," he husked. "There is nothing wrinkled about you. At least as far as I can determine at the moment. It will take a much more thorough inspection to be completely certain, however."

Charlie closed her eyes as she battled the poignant sweetness that flowed through her blood. Damn Marlow. He was the only man who had ever been able to make her melt in this terrifying manner. "Stop this," she demanded.

His lips continued to tease at her ear. "For a price."

"A price?"

"Will you halt your ridiculous attempts to interfere in my marriage to Miss Dashell?"

She stiffened in outrage, her gaze surging upward. So that was what this was all about. If he could not intimidate her in one manner, then he would use another.

A sudden, fierce fury burned away the trembling pleasure that had threatened to engulf her. "Why, you . . ."

"What?"

She lifted her hands to press against his hard chest. "Your fingers move one inch lower and I will blacken your eye."

He pulled back far enough to offer a mocking smile. "It would not be the first lump you have given me. Are you prepared to be reasonable?"

"You are a detestable wretch," she gritted.

"You have not answered my question, Charlie."

She did not even hesitate. "No."

The dark eyes flared before his head swiftly lowered and he claimed her lips in a bold, utterly possessive kiss.

Chapter Four

"Lord Marlow, whatever have you done to your eye?"

Feeling himself blush for the first time in nearly a decade, Marlow carefully escorted Miss Dashell through the vast crowd that filled Vauxhall.

He supposed it had been a forlorn hope that the darkness of the pleasure gardens would disguise the swollen blackness of his eye. It seemed to be a source of interest and amusement wherever he went.

Blast Charlie.

His lips momentarily thinned with annoyance. Perhaps it was not entirely her fault. After all, he was the one who had initiated the heated kiss. And it had been his choice to tug her into his arms so that he could feel her slender softness pressed to his oddly aching body. But when she had so readily parted her lips and even moaned in pleasure, he could not have suspected that she would so abruptly lose her nerve.

With mind-numbing speed she had gone from an eager participant in the kiss to a frantic virgin. He had barely had time to adjust to the change when she was desperately pressing against his chest in denial, her clenched hand slipping upon the satin smoothness of his coat and jerking up to smash him directly in the eye.

Embarrassed by the entire fiasco, Marlow had been forced to slink out the back door.

He never should have kissed the wench, he told himself a hundred times over the next two days. Not only had he behaved as a churlish brute, but her passionate response had left him achingly, fiercely aroused.

And even worse was the knowledge that for all his aggravation and impatience with Charlie, if he had the opportunity again, he would not hesitate to taste of her sweetness.

Which was precisely why he had so cleverly altered his plans for Friday evening. He could not properly concentrate upon Miss Dashell with Charlie near. Not only did she manage to rile his temper without even trying, but she was bound to bring along that worthless fribble of a brother.

And of course, there was the ever-present danger he might lose all sense and give in to the desire that smoldered relentlessly within him.

Flinching inwardly at the memory of just how delicious Charlie had felt in his arms, Marlow sternly trained his thoughts upon the young maiden at his side. *Blast it all*. He had known for years that Charlie could stir his passions. He had known it from that moment in the hayloft. She also managed to infuriate, aggravate, and drive him noddy.

If he were to think of kissing any maiden, it should be this one at his side. Perhaps she would not make his stomach clench in need nor his nights a blaze of longing misery, but he very much doubted that she would blacken a gentleman's eye.

A brief glance at the elderly Dashells assured him that they were content to allow his servants to see them safely to the box he had rented. Taking Miss Dashell's fingers, he firmly placed them upon his arm and with the skill of an acknowledged rake smoothly led her toward the darkened walkways. Before this evening was out, Miss Dashell would have no doubt that she was being courted.

No doubt whatsoever.

Too innocent to realize his intent, the golden-haired angel willingly followed his lead, although there was a faint frown upon her brow.

"My lord, you have not told me how you were injured."

"A trifling incident," he kept his tone determinedly light. "Nothing to concern you, my dear."

"You have not been in a . . . brawl, have you?" she demanded, making Marlow wonder precisely what Charlie had said of him. No doubt she had painted him the worst sort of scoundrel.

"No, simply an unfortunate encounter with a crazed ruffian," he muttered.

"Dear heavens, do not say you were accosted upon the streets of London?"

"Let us just say that a gentleman is hardly safe to leave his chambers." He easily sidestepped a large group of dandies and tugged her ever deeper into the gardens. "Ah, here is the famous walk."

"Oh, how charming." She glanced curiously about the various gardens and follies that lined the shadowed walk. "May I make a confession?"

"But of course, my dear."

She offered a dimpled smile. "I am very glad that your cousin had bespoken your theater box. I far prefer the pleasures of Vauxhall."

"Yes," he smiled in return. "I thought you might."

"It is a pity, however, that Miss Rowe was unable to join us."

Marlow's smile faded. He had deliberately waited until late this afternoon to send Charlie a note informing her that he must cry off from his invitation to the theater. He had also deliberately avoided mentioning that he had altered his arrangements to take Miss Dashell to Vauxhall. He did not want the wench about to spoil his plans.

"A great pity," he managed to lie without biting his tongue. "In her absence, I hope that I shall prove to be a sadly inferior but bearable companion."

"How silly. You are always a delightful companion."

Her words were precisely what were expected of a maiden. Just as she walked with the proper distance between them, and smiled at the suitable moments.

It was all perfect. Without a trace of warmth or genuine pleasure.

"I wonder."

She blinked at his muttered words. "Whatever do you mean, sir?"

"It is very difficult to determine, my dear, whether you truly prefer my presence or merely tolerate my attentions."

"What maiden would not be honored to receive your attentions, my lord?" she obediently mouthed, then her eyes widened with sudden delight. "Oh look, a juggler."

Marlow nearly growled his frustration. Was the maiden playing coy? Or was she genuinely more interested in a juggler than his own attempts at romance? A juggler who was frankly pitiful.

"How charming."

Miss Dashell watched the fumbling entertainer for a long moment. Then, glancing up at his impatient countenance, she gently cleared her throat.

"Perhaps we should return to my parents?"

Marlow gritted his teeth. He had drawn this maiden aside with a purpose. He was not going to be bested by a bloody juggler.

"In a few moments." He forced his expression to gentle lines. "You have yet to see the Hermit."

There was a moment before she gave a faint nod of her head. "Very well."

With a faint tug he had her moving ever further from the mingling crowd and deeper into the shadows. Even the blare of the band became muted. Almost casually he pulled her closer, hoping that perhaps the warmth of her body or the scent of her skin would stir his waning interest.

"It is a beautiful evening, is it not?"

"Oh yes, quite beautiful."

" 'A woman's face with nature's own hand painted, hast thou the master mistress of my passion . . .' " he softly quoted.

The fair brows drew together in puzzlement. "What was that?"

He nearly stumbled over his feet at her question. How could any educated maiden not recognize the greatest of bards? Surely she had possessed a governess to see to her learning?

Then he sternly chastised his harsh judgment. He should be pleased she was not a bluestocking, should he not? "Shakespeare."

"Oh." She offered a pretty grimace. "I fear I have never taken much interest in such studies."

"I see. May I be so bold as to ask what are your interests?"

"Well . . . dancing, of course."

"Certainly." He regarded her beautiful features. "Every maiden loves to dance."

"And jackstraws," she continued. "Oh, and charades. I adore charades. Do you?"

A chill inched down his spine. Jackstraws? Charades? Against his will he recalled Charlie's accusing words. *She's barely out of the nursery . . .*

Damn it all. He gave a shake of his head. His own father was a good ten years his mother's senior, and they had a perfectly normal marriage. Many gentlemen married women younger than themselves.

Miss Dashell was eighteen and firmly placed upon the Marriage Mart. He was simply unaccustomed to innocent maidens. That was all.

"It has been some years since I attempted charades," he hedged.

The dimples danced. "We often play after dinner, if you would care to join us some evening."

Marlow resisted the urge to shudder. "Yes, perhaps."

"I will tell Mother to send you an invitation."

Coming to an abrupt halt, Marlow firmly took her hands in his own. He was weary of coy games. He desired to know precisely what this maiden thought of him. "Miss Dashell."

The blue eyes were lovely but unreadable as she met his steady gaze. "Yes?"

"I wish to . . ."

"'Ello, luv." The strident female voice echoed through the perfumed air with a rasping edge. Startled by the unexpected interruption, Marlow turned his head to discover a blowsy, heavily painted female swaying in his direction. "Thought you could hide from me, did you?"

His nose thinned with distaste at the shabby gown that was cut to reveal a disgusting amount of the large bosom and at the suspiciously red curls that bobbed about the poxed countenance. "Ma'am, I do not know you, but this is a proper lady. I will thank you to keep your distance," he warned in cold tones.

Far from frightened by his chilling demeanor, the trollop gave a snort of laughter and swayed even closer. "A proper lady, is she? Well, then mayhap she gives her favors for free. Us working girls has to be paid for our services. You owe me a farthing."

Marlow wondered if the woman was foxed. Or perhaps she was simply unhinged. It was not uncommon among the poor street prostitutes.

His brief distraction, however, came to a swift end when he realized that Miss Dashell was regarding him with a horrified expression.

"My lord?" she questioned softly.

"'Tis nothing, my dear," he retorted in sharp tones, oddly disturbed that she would believe for even a moment he would choose to be intimate with this doxy. "The woman is obviously demented."

The woman slapped her hands onto her wide hips and leered openly at him. "You didna seem to think me demented last evening when you asked me to spread me . . ."

"Enough," he growled, his countenance flushed with anger and embarrassment. "Come along, Miss Dashell."

"Rot yer soul," the woman called in rough tones. "Make a poor woman starve after having yer wicked way with her."

Taking the shocked maiden's arm in a firm grip, Marlow marched them back down the path without a backward glance. Of all the hideous, vexing luck. Was fickle fate against him? Was he ever to have a moment alone with Miss Dashell so that he could press his sadly faltering suit?

"My lord," a soft voice broke into his dark thoughts, "perhaps you should offer the woman some payment. I should not like to think of her being hungry."

He glanced down with smoldering impatience. "I do not allow myself to be blackmailed by common tarts."

Her lips thinned. "But, sir, if you . . ."

"I certainly did not," he snapped, any thought of romance now completely destroyed. Indeed, he only wanted this wretched evening to be done with. "I have never seen that woman before she so rudely interrupted us."

"Very well," she muttered, although she did not sound as if she were entirely convinced of his innocence.

His teeth ground until he thought they might crack. "Come, they will soon have the fireworks display."

Returning Miss Dashell to her speculative parents, Marlow discovered himself barely capable of playing the role of gracious host. Hardly surprising. It was bad enough that his entire scheme to lure Miss Dashell alone had been ruined. But to now have her wondering if he were the sort to dally with alleyway prostitutes went beyond the pale.

He stewed in the darkened corner, not even aware of the fireworks that filled the air. The only bright spot of the entire evening was the fact that Charlie had not been here to see the humiliating encounter. How she would have chuckled and crowed to see him being badgered by the daft jade. It would have been better than the farce he had forced her to miss.

Charlie . . .

Marlow slowly stiffened.

No. It was not possible. Not only could she not have known that he would be at Vauxhall this evening, but not even she could be so foolish as to have risked her reputation to discover such a lowly prostitute to humiliate him.

Could she?

Recalling the fiery combination of lust and fury in her eyes when she had struggled free of his tight embrace, his certainty began to waver. There could be no doubt that she had been humiliated by her ready response to his kiss. And that she regretted revealing such a tantalizing vulnerability.

Then for him to cleverly outwit her by bringing Miss Dashell to Vauxhall . . . surely it would have been the final straw.

His eyes slowly narrowed. It should have been unthinkable that Charlie was involved in such a nefarious scheme, but as the fireworks filled the night sky and Miss Dashell twittered with delight, his heart smoldered with growing suspicion.

It was quite late when Charlie at last slipped into a deep sleep.

She attempted to assure herself that her hours of tossing and turning were entirely due to her excitement over discovering a means of besting Marlow. After all, it had been quite clever of her to think of ruining his evening in such a scandalous fashion. She had no doubt that Miss Dashell and her parents would forbid him ever to come near her again.

Which, of course, meant that Tom would at least have a fighting chance to attract her attention.

But while her brave assurances seemed reasonable enough, there was an annoying voice in the back of her mind that kept reminding her that this was not her first sleepless night.

Since Marlow's devastating kiss, she had devoted far too many hours to considering the disturbing sensations he had stirred to life. Sensations she had thought dead and buried years ago. Sensations that a spinster firmly upon the shelf had no business experiencing.

At last weariness prevailed over the troubling memories and she slipped into an exhausted slumber, so exhausted that she did not stir when her window was pushed open, nor when the soft tread of footsteps neared her bed. Not even when a large form hovered over her reclined body for a long moment.

There was, indeed, no warning until her blessed sleep was splintered by a shock of icy water being poured over her head.

Sputtering and squawking in alarm, Charlie bolted upright. What had occurred? Had the sky fallen? Had the roof sprung a leak? Had . . .

With frantic hands she hastily wiped the water from her eyes to regard a dark male form that loomed dangerously over her bed. In his hand was the ceramic pitcher from the washstand.

Her expression froze in fury.

No, the sky had not fallen. It was much, much worse.

"Marlow," she rasped in angry disbelief. "Have you lost your mind?"

Tossing the empty pitcher onto the bed he planted his hands upon his hips. "Be happy I did not put you across my knee and give you the spanking you deserve."

"Spanking?" She struggled to clear her foggy mind. "What are you speaking of? You cannot walk into my private chamber and threaten . . ."

"Obviously, I can," he mocked.

She shivered as the icy cold water trickled down her spine. It was stark, unmistakable proof this was no horrible nightmare.

"This is madness, Marlow," she charged. "If you are discovered, we shall both be plagued by scandal."

He did not even flinch at her warning. Instead he leaned forward, a shaft of moonlight revealing the harsh lines of his expression.

"Then you shall have to ensure we are not discovered. You can begin by keeping that vitriolic tongue of yours under control."

Charlie abruptly sensed the tension that coiled through the air—a tension that came directly from the towering form above her. With a swift motion she was off the bed and backing away from her midnight intruder.

"Stop this. I insist that you leave."

He stalked forward, backing her against the wall. Even then he was not satisfied. With a swift motion, he planted his hands on either side of her head, easily trapping her.

"Not until I have achieved what I came for," he threatened in low tones.

Charlie regarded him with a growing unease. "And what is that?"

"Vengeance."

Chapter Five

Marlow glared down at the pale face. For hours he had brooded upon the moment he could properly send Miss Dashell upon her way so that he could seek out this aggravating minx. And even now the fury still poured like molten lava through his tense body. Ridiculously, however, as he regarded the woman who was stubbornly meeting him glare for glare, he discovered himself sharply aware of the warm, slender form so temptingly close to his own. Even the soft scent of her soap threatened to distract him.

No, Marlow, he warned himself sternly. *Not that.* He was here to ensure that Charlie realized the danger of interfering in his life. Not to remind himself just how desperately he desired her.

Almost as if aware of the sudden prickles of heat flaring between them, Charlie uneasily pressed herself against the wall.

"Vengeance?" she demanded in hoarse tones.

His lips thinned. "Oh, do not attempt to play coy with me, Charlie. I know quite well that you sent that harlot to Vauxhall."

"What? Do not be absurd," she attempted to bluster,

a revealing blush staining her cheeks. "Why would I send a harlot to Vauxhall?"

"To humiliate me, of course," he gritted.

"Good heavens, it is hardly my fault if a harlot . . ."

"Enough," he growled, his anger returning full force at the memory of the ghastly doxy. He would be fortunate if Miss Dashell ever spoke with him again. "You cannot lie or wiggle out of this one. I know quite well you were responsible for that woman. Who was she?"

She flinched at the dangerous edge in his voice. "I . . ."

"The truth, Charlie."

The vixen fought a silent battle before grudgingly heaving a sigh. "An actress."

"Well, I suppose I should be thankful that you did not actually enter the stews to seek out a prostitute."

"Of course I did not."

He smiled without humor at her shocked tone. "I would put nothing beyond you. I hope she cost you a fortune. She was very convincing."

She shifted in discomfort. "The cost was of no importance."

"Of course not." He leaned even closer, his gaze piercing deep into her wide eyes. "The only thing important was making a fool of me, was it not?"

"No, I simply wished Miss Dashell to realize that you are an incurable rake. She deserves a husband who will be faithful to her."

His brows snapped together at her insult. Why, the meddlesome wench. How dare she presume to know what he would or would not do.

"And how do you know I will not be faithful?" he charged.

The delicate features hardened into a disdainful mask. "Unlike Miss Dashell, I am not a starry-eyed innocent. I know quite well you have kept a string of beautiful mistresses. I believe the latest one is known as Aphrodite."

Marlow gave a choked cough of embarrassment. Dash it all, could a gentleman have no secrets in this damnable town? It was not as if he flaunted his beautiful courtesans. Or even escorted them about London. How the devil could Charlie be so intimately acquainted with his private life?

More than a tad disconcerted at the thought of this maiden realizing his most sordid secrets, he struggled to regain command of the confrontation. "I would think that a proper maiden would know better than to listen to such ill-bred gossip," he retorted.

Her brows lifted in a superior fashion. "Do you mean to imply that you do not have a mistress?"

"I mean to imply that no decent lady should concern herself with such matters."

"Not even your wife?"

He swallowed a growl of impatience. What did this woman know of Society marriages? Of course she would demand utter fidelity in her husband. She was a passionate, spirited maiden who would give her entire heart and soul into a relationship. Miss Dashell, however, was not the same sort. He ruefully considered the young maiden's distant, almost aloof demeanor. She would no doubt be eager to have her husband seek his pleasure elsewhere. "That is none of your concern."

"You refuse to answer because you have no intention of giving up your lady birds," she shrilly accused.

"Damn it, Charlie, I will not have you interfering," he snapped, fiercely disliking the vague shadow of guilt she was stirring to life. "Miss Dashell will be my wife."

Her gaze narrowed as her own ready temper flared.

"Even though you are bound to make her miserable? You do not love her. You do not even desire her."

"And Tom does?" he ruthlessly returned.

"He will at least treat her with respect and kindness."

Marlow gave a short, mocking laugh. He was far too familiar with Tom to believe for a moment that he would make any maiden anything but wretched.

"When he bothers to notice her at all. Good God, he cannot even be bothered to court her properly. Instead, he depends upon you to win his bride. I suppose that you intend to join their household so that you can remind your brother to leave his paintings and occasionally join his wife in her bed?"

She readily bristled at his condemning tone, although the manner in which she bit her lip assured him that he had struck a nerve. "You need not be so crude."

He regarded her in sardonic disbelief. "Crude? This from a woman who hired an actress to play the role of a harlot to accost me?"

She hunched a shoulder in a defensive motion. "You should not have attempted to cut Tom out. It was a devious trick."

Marlow paused, struck by a sudden puzzlement. "How did you know that I would be at Vauxhall?"

"I . . ." She licked her full lips. "Miss Dashell told me."

"Impossible. She did not know of my plans until less than an hour before she joined me."

Her lashes lowered to cover her expressive eyes. A certain indication she was about to utter an untruth.

"I asked her maid."

Exasperated by her evasiveness Marlow curled his fingers beneath her chin and forced her countenance up to meet his glittering gaze.

"Charlie."

"Oh, very well," she snapped. "I suspected that you intended to meet with Miss Dashell without me so I hired Miss Hake and followed you in a closed carriage."

Marlow stiffened in disbelief. "Are you mad?"

"No, just determined that you will not seduce Miss Dashell from Tom."

He regarded the features that were so familiar. Gads, he knew that she was protective of her brother, but this was ridiculous. To hire an actress and follow him through the streets of London? It was the behavior of a lunatic. Or . . . his eyes abruptly narrowed. Or a woman obsessed with a particular gentleman.

Without even being aware of his movements Marlow softened his grip upon her chin, allowing himself to appreciate the satin softness of her skin beneath his touch.

"And that is all?" he demanded, his voice sounding oddly thick in the darkness.

She sucked in a sharp breath, as if sensing the heat that tingled through his blood. "What do you mean?"

His gaze swept over her countenance and then lowered to the slender, shadowed form. His heart came to a halt. Dear heavens, the damp night rail had molded to her curves with a shattering precision. Even in the darkness he could detect the perfect swell of her breasts and the slender waist. His own body reacted with an instinctive surge of excitement.

"We both know that there are dozens of proper maidens who would suit Tom as well as Miss Dashell," he rasped, his fingers moving to stroke the tantalizing line of her neck. "Obviously it matters little to him which one you might chose."

She stirred beneath his touch, inwardly battling the sweet temptation that was smoldering in the darkness.

"I believe that Miss Dashell is best suited to make Tom happy."

"And more importantly you do not want her to be my wife. I do not believe you desire any woman to be my wife."

She frowned at his words. "Certainly I would pity any maiden foolish enough to tie herself to you."

"Pity or envy?" he demanded in husky tones.

"Envy?" Her features tightened. "Ugh. You are truly a most pompous toad."

He laughed softly at her fierce words, his fingers deliberately sweeping down her throat and over the satin swell of her breast. "Perhaps, but I also am wise enough to recognize when a maiden is behaving like a desperate fool. You would never go to such outlandish lengths if it were another gentleman who was wooing Miss Dashell." He carefully watched her eyes darken in reaction to his caress. "No, my dear. You cannot bear the thought of me wedding Miss Dashell, can you?"

Her breath rasped through the thick air. "You are daft. I dislike you intensely."

"Shall I prove otherwise?" he whispered.

"What?"

"This . . ."

Chapter Six

Charlie wanted to protest. She wanted to shove him aside and assure him that she thought him the most wretched of creatures. Above all she wanted to inform him that she could not care less if he wed every maiden in London, in all of England, as long as it was not Miss Dashell.

But the outraged words were effectively halted when the warm male lips covered her own. And they disappeared entirely as he firmly gathered her in his arms and folded her against the searing heat of his body.

She did not want to think. Or be bothered with pesky worries. Not when he was devouring her lips with a desperate hunger and his hands were running a restless path down her spine.

An urgent need clenched deep within her. This was Marlow. The man who aggravated her beyond bearing. The man who was currently threatening Tom's happiness. The man who had dared to sneak in her chambers and pour water over her head.

And yet, in his arms, he was the boy who had always been her closest companion. The friend who knew her deepest secrets. The neighbor she had desired for what seemed to be an eternity.

With a low moan, she arched closer to his solid muscles. A golden fire was burning through her body, filling the dark, empty places of her soul.

"Charlie." His lips eased to brush over her flushed cheeks. "You taste so sweet. So damnably sweet."

"Marlow . . . we should not," she managed to mutter.

He moved to lightly nibble at her ear. "I know."

She shivered in pleasure. "We do not even like one another."

"Like?" That disturbing mouth continued its delicious exploration, discovering a particularly sensitive hollow just below her jaw. "That is far too tepid a word for what lies between us, Charlie. We may wrangle and aggravate and torment one another, but we will always be a part of one another. Do you not feel it?"

Charlie battled a wild desire to laugh. How could she not feel it? Tangled in his arms with his lips sending pure magic through her heart, she could not possibly ignore the realization that she had never experienced anything so wonderfully right.

"I do not want this," she whispered even as her hands smoothed up his arms to grasp at his shoulders.

His rueful laugh sent a blaze of sensation over the bare skin of her neck. "And you imagine I do?" He tenderly pressed his lips to the pulse beating wildly at the base of her throat. "I have been battling the urge to bed you since I was eighteen. After tonight I shall no doubt go mad from wanting you."

Charlie squeezed her eyes shut at the sheer pleasure that rushed through her. She had to halt this. Soon she would be beyond reason, beyond caring for anything but that Marlow ease the sharp ache that clawed within her. "Marlow."

"What?" he demanded in abstracted tones, his clever hands slowly tugging her night rail upward.

"We must halt."

He continued to pull the satin of her night rail ever upward. "In a moment."

Despite her innocence, Charlie was well aware that a moment might be too late. Already her stomach was quivering in anticipation of his hands upon bare skin. One more kiss, one more caress, and they would be plunged into disaster.

"What of Miss Dashell?" she forced herself to mutter.

Marlow froze at her words, a fine shiver racing through his tense body. Just for a moment his arms tightened about her as if he would not be denied, his breath rasping through the thick silence. Then, without warning, he was abruptly stepping away to run his fingers roughly through his hair. "Damn you, Charlie."

Oddly chilled by his sudden withdrawal, Charlie wrapped her arms about her shivering form. "I think you should leave now."

He regarded her with a tight smile. "Leave? You believe we can just forget this?"

Forget? It was seared forever upon her mind. Still, she could not show weakness now. Not unless she was willing to give her innocence to a gentleman who fully intended to wed another.

"It must be forgotten. We have no choice," she retorted in tones surprisingly steady.

"There are always choices. It is all a matter of whether one is willing to pay the price." His gaze lowered to study her lips that were still warm from his kisses. "I am. Are you?"

Her eyes briefly closed as a sharp, unexpected flare of pain ripped through her heart. It was frightening how easy it would be to give in to temptation. She wanted to be in his arms. She wanted him to be the one to claim her innocence. She wanted . . . Marlow. Utterly and wholly.

The shock of the realization was enough to send her reeling against the wall, her head shaking in belated denial. "No. Please, no."

Marlow stilled at her fierce words, something that might have been pain tightening his features. "You need not panic, Charlie. I am no monster, no matter what you might think of me. I shall not press myself upon you."

"I . . ." On the point of assuring him that she would never fear such an absurd thing, Charlie halted. What could she say? That she had seen into her heart and realized the shocking truth? That she did not want him to leave? Not ever? "Please, Marlow, it is late. I only wish to return to bed."

He sucked in a deep breath. "Alone?"

"Yes."

"You can end this so easily? You can send me upon my way without a regret for what might be?"

She forced herself to meet his gaze squarely. "It is how it must be."

"No, it is how you are insisting that it must be." His dark eyes smoldered with suppressed emotion. "I am willing to remain and discover where this delicious encounter might lead."

"Marlow . . ." Her hand pressed to her tortured heart. "Please, do not."

His lips twisted in a humorless smile. "I see your mind is quite set. Then it appears there is nothing left to do but wish you sweet dreams."

He offered a mocking bow, then moved toward the open window. With athletic ease, he was over the sill and climbing down the trellis. Charlie instinctively moved to ensure that he made his way down safely, only to firmly halt her impulsive concern.

Marlow was going to marry Miss Dashell. Despite all her efforts to mar his courtship, she did not believe for a moment that the maiden was capable of resisting his potent charm. And why should she?

With a vague sense of nausea Charlie moved toward the bed. She did not note the clammy wetness of the sheets as she lay down. Or the chill in the air from the open window.

Instead she closed her eyes and breathed deeply of the lingering scent of Marlow's warm body.

It was barely past mid morning when Charlie firmly marched up the walk to the Dashells' elegant town house.

After a sleepless night, she had arisen to watch the pale crimson of dawn creep across the sky. It was not only the searing memory of the feel of Marlow's kisses that had kept her awake, but the knowledge that he had seen so easily into her heart.

She had not desired to see him wed to Miss Dashell, she had grudgingly acknowledged. Or, in truth, any other maiden. In the very depths of her soul she had believed that Marlow would always belong to her. Her friend, her tormentor, her lover. It was little wonder she had taken such pains to ensure that his courtship was doomed to failure.

After restless hours and a great deal of effort, she at last forced herself to face what must be done. And once the decision had been made she was anxious to put the unpleasant task behind her.

Which, of course, explained why she was standing upon Miss Dashell's stoop well before it was the proper hour for a visit.

Not allowing herself time for second thoughts, she grimly rapped upon the knocker and allowed the butler to usher her through the house to the private back salon.

At her entrance, Miss Dashell rose to her feet and offered a sweet smile. Even though the hour was early, the young maiden appeared lovely and rather gallingly well rested. Unlike herself, she acknowledged with a pang of envy. One glance in the mirror this morning was enough to assure her that she looked precisely as haggard and undone as she felt.

With an effort, Charlie did not allow her smile to falter as she crossed to stand before the maiden. "Good morning, Miss Dashell."

"Miss Rowe, what a lovely surprise."

"I know that it is shockingly early, but I wished to visit with you before your horde of admirers arrived."

A charming blush touched Miss Dashell's alabaster cheeks. "Oh, what a tease you are. I hardly have a horde of admirers."

Charlie deliberately glanced about the room, which was nearly buried beneath the vast array of bouquets. Roses, tulips, orchids, and daisies all vied for attention. She could only wonder if there was a hothouse in all of London that had not been stripped bare.

"Oh, I would say definitely a horde," she murmured, returning her gaze to the beautiful countenance. Gads, it was no wonder that Marlow desired her as his wife. Her heart wrenched in loss. "You are quite the Toast of the Season."

The young maiden appeared modestly flustered by

the praise. "Everyone has been very kind. Will you have a seat?"

"Thank you." Charlie moved to perch upon the edge of a delicate chair, her expression determined as Miss Dashell settled upon the nearby sofa. "I hope you had a pleasant evening with Lord Marlow?"

"Oh yes, we went to Vauxhall," the maiden breathed, her eyes shining with remembered pleasure. "It was just as charming as I hoped it would be, and the fireworks quite took my breath away. We did, of course, miss your companionship."

Charlie mustered a thin smile. It was the moment. She could not balk now. "I fear that I was unavoidably detained. I . . . did hear that there was an unpleasant incident while you were in the gardens."

"Incident?" It took a moment before the maiden grimaced in displeasure. "Oh . . . the poor . . ."

"Yes," Charlie firmly interrupted the embarrassed words. "Most unfortunate. I fear that you must have been quite overwrought."

"Not nearly so overwrought as Lord Marlow," she confessed in surprisingly dry tones.

"Ah, yes. No doubt."

The displeasure only deepened. "I am not so innocent that I do not realize that there are those gentlemen who enjoy the company of such females. Still, it is not pleasant to have it so openly flaunted."

"No, you are mistaken," Charlie retorted sharply.

Miss Dashell blinked in mild surprise at the fierce tone. "I beg your pardon?"

Charlie felt nearly ill as she gave a shake of her head. How could she ever have sunk so low? Marlow was right. Her actions had been that of an obsessed, desperate madwoman. "It is not what you think, Miss Dashell," she admitted in low tones.

"I am sorry, I do not understand."

She sucked in a deep breath and squared her shoulders. "I . . . I have learned that the incident last night was no more than a lark being played upon Lord Marlow."

"A lark?" Miss Dashell demanded in understandable shock.

Charlie battled a revealing blush. "You know how childish those of the *ton* can be," she hedged. "They no doubt thought it a grand jest to tease him by hiring the woman and having her accost him in your company."

"It is not a very amusing jest."

"No, it most certainly is not." Charlie glanced down at her tightly clenched hands. "I should say it was the behavior of a very spiteful child."

There was a long pause, and at last Charlie forced her gaze up to meet the slow, obviously relieved smile of Miss Dashell.

"I am glad that you revealed the truth. I did not like to think of Lord Marlow as being so indifferent to the plight of the poor woman."

Just for a hideous moment Charlie wanted to jump from the chair and shout that Lord Marlow was hers. That he needed a maiden with spirit who would keep him firmly in check, not a pliable, always easily swayed female who would constantly give in to his stronger will.

Only the memory of those miserable hours she had spent thinking of keeping Marlow from the woman he obviously preferred halted the trembling words.

It was not her place to interfere. Marlow was perfectly capable of choosing his own bride. And if he desired Miss Dashell, then she could do nothing more than gracefully step aside.

She bit her lip until she drew blood. "Lord Marlow can be arrogant and overbearing, but he does possess a good heart. And in truth, he is a very honorable gentleman."

Miss Dashell raised her brows at the unexpected praise. "Do you care for him, Miss Rowe?"

"I . . . of course I do. He is a very old friend."

The younger maiden considered for a moment before giving a slight nod of her head. "Then he must be a wonderful gentleman. You would chose no other for a friend."

"Yes, he is quite wonderful." Charlie abruptly rose to her feet. She had to get away from Miss Dashell before she embarrassed them both by bursting into tears. "I must be on my way."

Caught off guard by Charlie's abrupt announcement, Miss Dashell slowly lifted herself from the sofa. "You will not stay for tea?"

"And risk being trampled by your horde of admirers?" Charlie weakly teased, hoping she did not appear as sick at heart as she felt. "No, I believe it is best I return home. Good-bye, Miss Dashell."

Without even waiting for the maiden to reply, Charlie turned upon her heel and fled from the room.

She had done what she had set out to do. Miss Dashell was convinced that Marlow was a respectable, honorable gentleman who would make her a fine husband.

Now she needed to be alone to mourn a future that suddenly seemed wretchedly bleak.

Chapter Seven

Four hours later, Charlie secreted herself in the back garden to absently feed the numerous birds that played among the flower beds. As a rule, she found such surroundings a soothing balm to whatever may be troubling her. Nothing could seem quite so bad when the sun was shining and the air was filled with the sweet perfume of roses.

Today, however, her heart remained dark and troubled.

What did it matter if the sun was shining and the roses were blooming when her thoughts were filled with images of Marlow with the beautiful, utterly perfect Miss Dashell?

Would they wed before the end of the Season? Would she be forced to attend the ceremony and pretend that her heart was not breaking? Would the maiden soon be heavy with Marlow's child?

Charlie flinched and closed her eyes against the stabbing pain. Perhaps she should return to her home in Surrey, she acknowledged. At least there she would not be forever encountering Marlow. And in time she could reconcile herself to the knowledge that he was forever beyond her reach.

Best of all, there would be no one about to note that she was far from her usual cheerful self.

Yes, a few months in the country was just what she needed, she told herself, tossing out a handful of breadcrumbs.

"They shall soon be too fat to fly," a dark voice murmured from just behind her.

Nearly tumbling from the marble bench, Charlie jerked her head about to discover Marlow watching her with an unreadable expression.

Her heart swelled at the sight of his lean form attired in a crisp blue coat and silver waistcoat, his features unbearably handsome in the bright sunlight. This man had been a part of her life from the day she was born. How could she possibly lose him now?

Then, with an effort, she wrenched control of her painful emotions. Marlow wanted Miss Dashell as his bride. If she truly loved him, then she would do all in her power to ensure that he was happy.

No matter what the cost to herself. "Marlow. Whatever are you doing here?"

"Tom told me where I could find you."

She silently cursed her brother. Tom rarely left his studio long enough to know what day it was. How had he possibly realized she was in the garden? "I see."

There was an oddly awkward pause before Marlow cleared his throat. "Am I intruding?"

"No, of course not." She pasted a stiff smile to her lips. "Indeed, I am glad that you are here. I wished to speak with you."

His own smile was wry as he moved to settle his large frame beside her upon the bench. "Then for once we are of one mind. A rare occurrence."

"Yes." She shivered at the feel of his hard thigh

brushing her own. She might have convinced her mind that Marlow belonged to another, but obviously her body was not so easily persuaded.

Almost as if able to sense her sharp reaction to his proximity, those wicked black eyes ran a piercing survey over her pale countenance. "You must have much upon your mind, my dear."

She stiffened in sudden fear. He could not have guessed her troubled feelings, not when she was just realizing them for herself. "Why do you say that?"

"You have always sought the solitude of the nearest gardens when you are troubled."

"Oh, yes. I suppose I do." She sucked in a relieved breath. She knew she could bear anything but his pity for her foolishness. "They are very soothing."

The elegant features abruptly softened. "I remember discovering you hidden in the midst of a lilac bush after you discovered your father had drowned. It took me hours to convince you to come out."

Charlie remembered as well. She had been shocked and devastated at the loss of her father. Time after time her mother had come to the garden to attempt to comfort her, but she had refused to speak with anyone but Marlow.

She offered him a rueful glance. "You told me that I would grow roots and be stuck forever in the garden if I remained any longer."

"What else could I do?" he demanded, a sudden sparkle entering the dark eyes. "You bit me when I reached into the bush to pull you out. I still have the scar."

Her eyes narrowed in disbelief. "You are jesting."

"Not at all." With swift movements Marlow removed his gloves to reveal the tiny, pale scar near his thumb. "You see?"

"Good heavens."

The dark eyes easily captured her startled gaze. "You well and truly put your mark upon me, my dear."

Her breath threatened to catch at the tenderness in his tone. "I did not realize that I was such a savage."

"You were in pain." With a smile he reached up to lightly touch the faint sickle-shaped scar just above her brow. "Besides which, I believe I left more than one scar upon you."

Charlie sharply bit the side of her tongue as a shower of pleasure flooded from his soft touch. "It was not your fault that I was ridiculous enough to jump off the roof of the stables," she muttered.

"It was I who dared you to do it."

"You also dared me to kiss the frog that you captured, but I was wise enough to push you in the pond instead."

He gave a low chuckle. "We also share many good memories, Charlie. How many hours did we spend fishing at the river or sneaking into the orchards to steal apples?" His fingers moved to trace down her cheek to the line of her jaw. "I recall entire days that we lay in the meadow and watched the clouds float past."

With a muffled moan, Charlie was on her feet and moving away from his agonizing touch. It was that or throw her arms about him and refuse ever to let go. "It all seems a very long time ago," she muttered.

There was a faint rustle, and then Marlow was standing beside her, his hands reaching out to firmly grasp her shoulders so that he could turn her to meet his searching gaze. "What is it, Charlie?" he demanded in low tones. "What is troubling you?"

She kept her gaze grimly trained upon the crisply knotted cravat, willing herself to be brave. Surely this was like pulling a tooth? Better over with in one swift jerk of agony. "I . . . owe you an apology."

"An apology?" he demanded in surprise.

"Yes. I have behaved in a most reprehensible manner."

His fingers abruptly tightened upon her shoulders. "Because of our kiss?"

The unexpected demand brought her head up in shock. "No, of course not."

"Then what?"

"I speak of my efforts to turn Miss Dashell from you."

A guarded expression descended upon the male countenance as he dropped his hands and stepped away. "I see."

Charlie frowned, uneasy at the odd stiffness that suddenly settled about Marlow. Surely he should be delighted by her confession? "I had no right to presume that you would not be a loving or kind husband. And I certainly had no right to make her believe you were less than honorable."

His gaze swept her face, the black eyes dark with a piercing intensity. "That is quite an admission. May I ask what has prompted your change of heart?"

"I realize how ridiculous I have been." She uneasily wrapped her arms about her waist. She knew Marlow better than anyone in the entire world. And yet, at this moment she was incapable of sensing what thoughts were churning behind that somber expression. "I cannot force the poor maiden to care for Tom. She must be allowed to follow the dictates of her own heart."

Charlie thought she heard the sharp intake of his breath, although it was impossible to determine for certain. "So you will no longer stand in my way?"

"No." She bravely kept the pain from her voice. "Indeed, I visited Miss Dashell early this morning and assured her that the woman who accosted you last evening was no more than a poor jest designed to embarrass you. I also assured her that you would be quite a wonderful husband. I do not doubt that you will find her perfectly prepared to accept your offer."

Once again he caught her off guard as his brows drew together and his lips thinned with what appeared for all the world as fury. "It would not trouble you if I wed Miss Dashell?" he snapped.

Blast it all. What did he want from her? Had he not been the one to ring a peal over her for daring to interfere in his relationship with Miss Dashell? And had he not already made it painfully clear he intended to make the maiden his bride?

Why the devil would he behave as if she had somehow deeply insulted him by doing precisely what he desired?

It was obvious she simply could not please him, no matter how she might try, she told herself with a jaundiced flare of self-pity.

"I believe you could make no finer choice," she forced herself to retort. "She is gentle, with a pleasing manner, and, of course, astonishingly beautiful. I daresay you shall be the envy of every gentleman in London when you appear with her upon your arm."

"Oh, yes." His lips twisted. "She is quite perfect."

Charlie flinched as if he had physically struck her. Indeed, she would have preferred a blow to the sharp ache that clawed at her heart. She very much feared it was a pain that would not soon be eased. "Then I suppose it is settled," she said in dull tones.

There was a brief pause before Marlow gave a deep growl. "Is it?"

She frowned in wary confusion. "What do you mean?"

He stepped sharply forward, his hands once again reaching up to grasp her shoulders. "You may have put from your mind what occurred between us last night, but I assure you I have not. It has haunted me since I left you."

Charlie clenched her hands in shock. At last she was beginning to comprehend his odd behavior. Dear heavens, he was feeling guilty at what had occurred between them last night, she acknowledged. Not only feeling guilty, but clearly determined to somehow make reparations for his overly bold intimacies.

No. Her stomach clenched in distaste. As easy as it would be to allow his troubled conscience to lure him into her clutches, she knew it would bring nothing but regrets for both of them.

Whatever his desire for her, Marlow had chosen Miss Dashell to be his wife. His future had been clearly decided before she had so rudely intruded. Her love could not overcome the resentment he was bound to feel at her part in the end of his dream.

Bravely battling the ever ready tears, she managed to meet his smoldering gaze without balking.

"Then you should put it from your mind," she said in firm tones. "It was a moment of madness, nothing more."

His nose flared with annoyance. "Madness? Perhaps. But that does not alter the fact that I very nearly seduced you."

"I . . . but you did not."

"Not from lack of trying," he pointed out in grim tones.

Heat filled her cheeks. His words were recalling dangerous sensations. The soft darkness that had wrapped about them as he had hungrily plundered her lips. The damp silk that had clung to her sensitive skin. The heat of his hard body that promised such tantalizing paradise.

A sweet, renegade flare of need rushed through her. Even now, when she was struggling to do what was best for both of them, she was consumed by desire. "Marlow, this is absurd," she breathed, knowing that she must bring an end to this encounter. Perhaps someday she would be able to meet him without being consumed by her fierce emotions. But not now. "What occurred last evening was a mistake. It is best that we both put it from our minds and continue with our plans for the future."

"And what plans would those be?" he rasped.

"I shall continue caring for Tom, and you shall wed Miss Dashell."

He regarded her as if he had never truly seen her before. "And that is what you desire?"

Charlie swallowed a hysterical urge to laugh. He would flee in horror if she revealed what she desired. "Of course."

The black eyes flared as he stepped back, his hands clenching into fists at his side. At last he appeared convinced that she had no intention of allowing him to martyr himself for a brief flare of passion that meant nothing. At least to him.

"Then I shall not trouble you further." He offered a brief bow before he turned about and headed back up the path.

Instinctively Charlie reached out her hand to halt his retreat, only to force it back to her side.

He was now able to go to Miss Dashell with a clear conscience and nothing to concern him but how soon they could wed.

All there was left for her to do was pack her bags and return to Surrey.

Chapter Eight

Marlow was in an utter state of despair.

Having devoted the week to every form of distraction he could conjure, he was at last secluded in his library, a bottle of brandy his only companion. His clubs could not hold his interest, or the card tables, or dance floors, or the racetrack. Not even the thrill of searching for a new mistress could hold any appeal. His dissipation had done nothing more than leave him with a thick head and a surly temper that had frightened off all but his stoic servants.

He was well and truly miserable, he acknowledged as he swallowed a fiery gulp of the brandy. And only with the vaguest of hopes that time would eventually lessen the ache that burned with relentless determination in his heart.

Blast Charlie.

Blast her for handing him to Miss Dashell like a trussed pig for the slaughter when all he desired was to have Charlie in his arms, in his home, in his . . . life. Blast her for attempting to fool herself that the passion they shared was no more than a passing madness. Blast her for leaving him aching and alone and wishing to goodness he had taken her in that hayloft so that she was well and truly his with no means of escape.

And most of all, blast himself for refusing to acknowledge the truth for so long.

How could he have been so blind? So witless as to have allowed his long friendship to keep him from realizing what was so shockingly, painfully obvious?

Reaching for the decanter, Marlow was abruptly halted from his task of becoming thoroughly foxed when the door to the library was rudely thrust open and the short, portly form of Sir Henry Hammonds entered the room. His black frown should have been enough to send any intruder fleeing, but with his usual lack of finer sensibilities, Henry merely ignored the obvious warning and glanced about the shadowed, rather stale chamber before running a disapproving survey over Marlow's sallow countenance and the tousled silver-gold curls.

"Zounds, your mother did not exaggerate. You are in a sorry state."

Struggling from his chair, Marlow glared at his unwelcome guest. "Henry, what the devil are you doing here?"

The gentleman's expression was jaundiced as he folded his arms over his barrel chest. "Well, it was not my notion, I assure you. Can't abide a meddler. Besides which, there was a particular beauty I desired to view at Tattersall's. Still, your mother is not a woman to be easily reined. Rather a tartar when she has the bit between her teeth."

Marlow gave a shake of his head, wondering if he had consumed more brandy than he realized. "My mother?"

"I say, you are in a bad way if you cannot recall your own mother." Henry offered a frown. "She is a tall woman with gray hair and a habit of ordering others about."

"Of course I have not forgotten my mother," Marlow

retorted, his hand lifting to massage the tense muscles of his neck. He was in no humor to be polite. His head hurt and his body felt as if it had gone a dozen rounds with Gentleman Jackson. All he wanted was his brandy and a measure of peace. "I simply do not comprehend what she has to do with your presence in my library."

"She commanded that I call upon you." His gaze became oddly piercing. "Understandable."

Marlow gave a snort. "It most certainly is not understandable. Why would she do such a daft thing?"

"Said you were going to ruin."

He stiffened in embarrassment. He barely recalled the brief encounter with his mother two days before. Hardly surprising, since he had just returned from a night at a particularly rowdy gambling hell. But surely he had not been so pathetic as that?

"Absurd," he growled in annoyance.

"Is it?" Henry deliberately cast a glance toward the coat that had long ago lost its pristine crispness and the cravat that had been pulled loose to hang about his neck. "Looks as if you've put yourself to pasture to me. A sad state, Marlow."

Marlow's hand dropped to his side to clench into a tight fist. The hint of pity in his friend's tone rasped dangerously against his pride.

"Damn it, Henry. I do not need a keeper. Unless you wish to join me in a drink, I would suggest that you continue on your way to Tattersall's."

Henry remained firmly planted in the center of the room as he heaved a woeful sigh. "Ghastly business."

"What?"

"Women." He gave a mournful shake of his head. "Contrary creatures who can destroy the most reasonable of gentlemen."

"Contrary?" Marlow gave a disgusted snort. That had to be the greatest understatement of all time. "Bloody impossible, more like it."

"A wise gentleman would avoid them like the plague."

On the point of agreeing with his cynical companion, Marlow discovered himself pausing. For all his pain, would he truly wish never to have had Charlie in his life? Would he have avoided those impassioned kisses that haunted his dreams? Would he have gone through his life never knowing the tender, heady, aggravating emotions that wracked him whenever she was near?

No. Whatever the future held, he could not regret the love that filled his heart and revealed what paradise could be.

"Or discover the proper woman and hold her so close she cannot escape," he murmured softly.

Deeply shocked by his friend's descent into madness, Henry gave a choked cough of disapproval. "Gads, you do have it bad."

"I . . ."

Whatever protest Marlow had been about to make was abruptly halted when the door to the library was once again thrust open. On this occasion it was the stiff form of his butler who entered the room and offered a proper bow.

"Pardon me, my lord, but you have a caller."

"Another one?" Marlow heaved a deep sigh. "Blast it all, has my mother gathered every loose screw in London to pester me?"

The servant cleared his throat, a faint hint of displeasure marring his wooden expression. "Actually, my lord, the caller is Miss Rowe."

Marlow froze in shock, his heart abruptly lodged in his throat. "Charlie? Good God. Where did you put her?"

"In the front parlor."

"I must go to her." He flashed a distracted glance toward his silent companion. "Henry, will you show yourself out?"

"Of course."

Barely registering his friend's response, Marlow was out the door and charging down the hall. He could not imagine what had brought Charlie to his home, but he knew that it must be severe indeed to have made her risk scandal in such a blatant fashion.

With the same hurried motions, he thrust open the door to the distinctly masculine parlor that offered several heavy walnut chairs and his prized collection of Roman coins. A swift glance revealed Charlie standing beside the bay window, her slender form delightfully outlined by the simple yellow gown.

Just for a moment he allowed himself the exquisite pleasure of drinking in her vivid beauty. Henry had been right. She was a purebred from the top of her glossy raven curls to the tips of her tiny feet. An elegant, passionate beauty who would grace any gentleman's home.

His heart gave a sharp tug of longing, even as Marlow shook his head. Now was not the time to indulge in his dark regrets. Charlie obviously needed him, and he would not fail her.

"Charlie," he murmured, crossing the carpet as she turned to regard him with shadowed eyes. "What are you doing here?"

Much to his shock, she reached out to grasp his hands in her own, an expression of concern etched onto the delicate features. "Oh, Marlow. I know it is wrong of me to come here, but I had to see you."

A flare of unease tightened his stomach. "Why? What has occurred?"

She stepped closer, surrounding Marlow in a cloud of her scented warmth. His teeth clenched as he struggled to keep his male instincts under firm control.

"You do not have to pretend with me, Marlow," she said in soft tones. "I am so terribly sorry."

He frowned at the odd words. "Sorry?"

"I know that I have not been the friend that I should have been over the past few weeks . . ." She bit her bottom lip before continuing. "No, it has been even longer than that, but I want you to know if you need someone to share your sorrow and disappointment, I am here."

Utterly at a loss, Marlow studied the pale countenance. He did not know if it was the brandy or the disturbing nearness of this woman, but he was finding it impossible to discern what the devil had Charlie so upset.

"I see," he hedged.

Her own gaze swept over his unshaven jaw and the tangled curls, lingering a painful moment upon the undoubted signs of his sleepless nights that circled his eyes.

"You look terrible," she muttered, her fingers squeezing his own tightly. "I could just wring that horrid maiden's neck. To think we could all have been so mistaken in her. She was not worthy of you, Marlow. And someday you will be grateful that you managed to escape her treacherous clutches."

Marlow frowned in bemusement, even as he savored the feel of her warm fingers clutching his own. "I fear, Charlie, that I must be unconscionably dense, but while I could not be more delighted to see you, I haven't the least notion of what has you in such a twit."

She gave a click of her tongue at his words. "You must not attempt to salvage your pride before me, Marlow. I know, despite all the efforts to disguise the ugly truth, that Miss Dashell attempted to flee to Gretna Green with her dance instructor."

For a full moment Marlow gazed at her in sheer disbelief. Then, without warning, he tilted back his head to laugh with rich enjoyment. "Of course," he chuckled, recalling his brief conversations with the young maiden. "How very obvious. She adores dancing, you see. I do hope the dance instructor also enjoys charades and jackstraws."

Clearly not comprehending the humor in the situation, Charlie regarded him with wary concern. "Marlow, have you been drinking?"

His amusement slowly faded as he gazed deep into the silver gray eyes. For the first time, he realized the significance of her hasty arrival at his home.

Surely a woman who felt nothing for him would not have endangered her reputation by rushing to be with him? It had to mean something. Could he dare to hope that she harbored some tenderness in her heart?

The thought was both frightening and exhilarating.

"Something certainly has muddled my mind," he muttered wryly.

"Did you desire her so much?" she asked in weak tones.

"Do you want the truth, Charlie?"

"I . . ." She hesitated, as if fearing what he might say, before giving a brave lift of her chin. "Yes."

"I do not care if Miss Dashell chooses to elope with every dance instructor in London," he informed her.

He could feel the faint ripple of shock tremble through her body.

"You are obviously hurt, but soon, Marlow . . ."

"Damn it, Charlie," he firmly interrupted, not about

to have her believing he was nursing a broken heart. At least not over Miss Dashell. "If I am hurt it is not because of anything Miss Dashell has done. I have not sought her company since the night we visited Vauxhall."

Her lovely eyes darkened with confusion as she struggled to accept his fierce denial. "What?"

His features softened as a rush of tenderness cascaded through him. He was done attempting to deny the feelings that he had harbored for this delicious woman for years. Whatever peculiar fear had kept them apart had to be put in the past. He could no longer bear to keep her at a distance.

"I was a fool," he confessed, gazing deep into her wide eyes. "An arrogant fool. I thought to choose a wife who would prove no disturbance to my selfish existence. A sweet, young, biddable maiden I did not love nor even desire. Miss Dashell has never been more than a convenient means to meet my promise to my mother that I would be wed before my thirtieth birthday."

She deliberately glanced toward the shadows that marred his countenance. "Then why are you so distraught by her betrayal?"

"I am not," he said simply. "I did not even know she had run off with her dance instructor until you told me."

"Oh." A faint hint of color stained her cheeks. "It seems that I have needlessly intruded. Forgive me."

Marlow lifted her hands to press them to his pounding heart. He desperately longed to kiss her, to tug her into his arms and assure himself that she was not yet another illusion come to torment him. How often had he pictured her in his home? Seated before the fire, or sharing breakfast with him, or warming his bed at night?

Unfortunately he knew that the moment was not yet right.

"Do not apologize, Charlie," he said in tones gruff with suppressed emotion. "I am very happy to have you in my home. Heaven knows I have imagined you here often enough over the past few weeks. I must say, however, I am surprised that you would reveal such concern for my welfare."

The blush oddly deepened upon her cheeks. "You are my friend. I did not like to think of you suffering."

"Your friend?"

"Yes."

"And nothing more?" he demanded.

Without warning she abruptly tugged her hands from his grasp and stepped back from his tense form. A wary, almost hunted expression tightened the fragile features. "I should leave."

Marlow bristled at the mere threat. Oh, no. He was not spending yet another week in purgatory. His poor heart had been shredded quite enough for one lifetime.

"Not yet, Charlie." He easily moved to block her path to the door. He was quite prepared to tie her to the chair if necessary. Or perhaps the bed . . . He shuddered and swiftly smothered the delectable thought. Not now. But later. Definitely later. "Are you not going to ask why I have been so wretchedly miserable for the past week? Do you wish to know why my mother has begun fearing for my sanity and my friends have learned to avoid my foul temper?"

She licked her lips in a nervous manner as she took an impulsive step backward. "Marlow."

Undeterred, Marlow stalked ever closer, not halting until she was firmly backed into the wall. Even then he took the precaution of placing a hand on either side of her head. He was not having her flee before they had settled this once and for all.

He somberly regarded her uncertain features with a fierce determination. "It is because of you, my dear."

"Me?" she breathed in disbelief.

"You. Only you."

"But . . . why?"

"Because I can no longer ignore the realization that you are the only woman I desire as my wife. The woman who has been my friend, my companion—the woman I desire so fiercely that I am nearly mad with wanting you."

He could hear the sharp rasp of her breath as she struggled to accept his blatant declaration.

"But I am forever annoying you," she at last managed to croak.

Marlow gave a soft chuckle, unable to deny the truth of her words. No one could deny they had been at odds for far too long. And no doubt would be at odds again in the future. They were both too strong willed not to cross swords upon occasion. "We have both devoted a great deal of effort to annoying one another. Why do you suppose that is, my dear?"

"Because you are arrogant and overbearing and . . ."

Her words faltered to a halt as he deliberately shifted his hand to cup her cheek. Marlow allowed his burning need to smolder frankly in his eyes. "And the gentleman you desire."

There was a long, aching silence and Marlow discovered himself unable to breathe until at long last she gave a reluctant nod of her head.

"Yes," she whispered.

"Oh my sweet," he groaned in acute relief. He had nearly sunk to his knees in fear. "I suppose our wrangles were inevitable. We had been friends for so long that neither of us was prepared for that day in the hayloft. That sudden passion frightened both of us. It is little wonder we so readily struggled to erect barriers between us."

A slow, utterly bewitching warmth began to shimmer in her eyes as she frantically searched his countenance for the truth of his feelings. "Marlow, what are you saying?"

"I am making a wretched bumble of this, am I not?" he admitted with a wry grimace. "I can only suppose it is because I have never uttered the words before."

"What words?" she demanded in an unsteady voice.

His fingers gently stroked the tantalizing silk of her cheek. "I love you."

She abruptly clutched at his coat, as if fearing her knees were about to give way. "You love me?"

He smiled gently into her stunned expression. "Utterly and irrevocably, my dear."

"Oh."

"Is that all you can say?" he teased softly. "Will you not put me out of my misery and admit that you love me as well?"

A glow of joy lit her features, although her smile was decidedly mysterious. "Are you so certain of me, then?"

His eyes briefly closed as he recalled the suffering he had endured over the past week. "No, my sweet. I am not at all certain."

Tentatively her hand lifted to touch his cheek. "Of course I love you, you wretched man. I have loved you all my life." Her lips trembled with her own tortuous memories. "You cannot know how difficult it was to promote a match between you and Miss Dashell. The poor maiden had done nothing, and yet I wanted nothing more than to scratch out her eyes."

Sheer, magical relief flared through Marlow as he

sucked in a deep breath. She loved him. His torture was over.

It seemed wondrously, delightfully impossible.

"Then why the devil did you attempt to make me think that my kisses meant nothing to you?" he growled even as his fingers drifted down the curve of her neck to the tempting plunge of her neckline. "I have been in agony for days."

She grimaced. "I thought that you were only being noble. I could not keep you from Miss Dashell if she was who you wanted. I only desired your happiness."

A decidedly wicked glint entered his eyes as his caresses became even more daring. "And now, Charlie? Do you still desire my happiness?" he asked with a seductive smile.

A revealing heat flared through her eyes as she readily curved her slender frame closer to his hungry body. "That all depends, Marlow." She boldly lifted her arms to wrap them about his neck. "What precisely is entailed in ensuring your happiness?"

Pure bliss raced through his blood as he wrapped his arms about her and slowly lowered his head toward her waiting lips. "Well, first you must tell me when we shall be wed. I warn you that it had best be as soon as possible. I have waited too long to have you as my wife."

Her eyes darkened with mounting pleasure. "I suppose that can be arranged. What else?"

"And then you must agree to tell me of your love every single day," he whispered, his lips brushing lightly over her lips in a teasing motion. "After waiting so long to hear the words, I have a desperate need to be reminded quite often."

"Very well," she softly moaned.

"And then . . ."

"What?"

"This."

Marlow tugged his beloved even closer. The remaining means of revealing his happiness was best done without words, he decided as his lips closed hungrily over her own.

Charlie, for once, agreed without complaint.

More Regency Romance
From Zebra